DANNY ORLIS

AND

ROBIN'S BIG MISTAKE

DANNY ORLIS

AND

ROBIN'S BIG MISTAKE

BERNARD PALMER

Danny Orlis and Robin's Big Mistake
© 2024 by Bernard Palmer
All rights reserved. First edition 1966.
Second edition 2024.

Cover image: Adobe Firefly
Character illustrations: John Ball
Editor: Charlene Miskimen

Aneko Press Youth

www.anekopress.com
Aneko Press, Life Sentence Publishing, and our logos are trademarks of Life Sentence Publishing, Inc.
203 E. Birch Street
P.O. Box 652
Abbotsford, WI 54405
JUVENILE FICTION / Religious / Christian / Action & Adventure
Paperback ISBN: 979-8-88936-032-2
eBook ISBN: 979-8-88936-033-9
10 9 8 7 6 5 4 3 2 1
Available where books are sold

CONTENTS

ROBIN GIVES IN

The night was cold and forbidding. It had started to snow earlier in the evening, and the temperature plunged to new lows for the season. Frost rimmed the windows at the Evans home and chilled the far reaches of the bedrooms.

Robin Evans had pulled into the garage a few minutes before, after letting Alex Smith out at his front door, and had hurried to her room. On the way she braced herself for the ordeal with her dad that was sure to come. Lately every time she stepped into the house when he was there, they had an argument. Fortunately this night he was either asleep or had decided he was too tired to give her trouble.

She undressed hurriedly in the cold room and crawled into bed. Her Bible lay, unread, on the stand nearby.

For a moment or two she stared up at the ceiling and thought about Alex. He was just about the most wonderful guy any girl could ever go out with. It still didn't seem possible to her that he would even look at her, let alone go out with her. Every other girl in school would be thrilled to have a chance to go out with him – or even to have him stop in the hall at school and talk for a minute.

If it just wasn't for the school dance. At the thought of the annual all-school dance an ache came to her heart. Alex insisted that she go with him, but she didn't really want to. As a Christian she knew she had no business there.

She rolled over on her side and closed her eyes for a moment. There was no use in being miserable about it. Alex would understand. He'd be kind, gracious, and gentlemanly, even if he was disappointed. That was the wonderful kind of guy he was.

She'd explain to him that she couldn't go with him because it was against her convictions. He'd understand. And even if he didn't, he thought so much of her that he wouldn't urge her to go. He'd probably even stay away himself.

She lay awake for an hour or more, going over exactly what she would say to him and anticipating his replies so she could work out her arguments. At last she drifted off to sleep.

The next day Robin saw Alex in the corridor at school the way she always did. She told him what she had decided. However, Alex didn't react at all the way she had thought he would.

"What do you mean, you're not going to go to the dance?" he echoed. "You promised me you would. Don't you remember? Or doesn't your word mean anything anymore?"

"Of course it does," she protested weakly, struggling for words. "But I–I've been thinking it over. I can't go, Alex. I–I just wouldn't feel right about it."

Anger clouded his eyes. "Well now, that's just too bad." He pulled in a quick breath. "Let me tell you something, young lady. I wouldn't feel right about going alone."

Her face blanched.

"It's too late now for me to find someone else – or is that the way you planned it?"

"I–I didn't mean to–to–" her voice died away, miserably.

"You might think you're going to stay at home, but you're not. You–you're going to go with me tonight, or you're not going out with me at all anymore."

Robin's gaze met his and pleaded desperately. "But, Alex," she continued, "I could hardly sleep last night. I–I wouldn't feel right about going to a dance. I know that as a Christian I don't have any right to go to a place like that."

"Who says you don't?" he demanded. His words were taut with anger. "Answer me that. I think you're just trying to get rid of me and you think this is as good a way as any."

"Alex!" She grasped his arm. "You know it's not that."

"Then go to the dance with me and prove it." His anger seemed to die away. "This is just some more of that stuff your parents have been telling you. They're trying to run every minute of your life, and they'll keep it up as long as they get away with it."

"It's not that," she retorted. "Not exactly."

"Do they want you to dance or don't they? Answer me that."

"Well, they don't like it, but–"

"Then you're going with me. Understand?"

It wasn't because Robin's parents objected that she didn't want to go to the dance with Alex, although they wouldn't like it if she did. She had convictions of her own. Convictions that wrenched at her heart. Convictions that had been ruining her sleep ever since she told Alex she'd go to the dance with him.

He took hold of her arm and squeezed it possessively.

"We don't want to let your parents spoil everything for us," he said. "They've just forgotten what it's like to be young and to want to have a little fun. That's the big trouble. They just don't understand."

She was a long while in answering.

"I–I really would rather stay home from the dance," Robin told him lamely.

"No, you wouldn't," Alex countered. "You're only saying that because your parents and that narrow preacher of yours have gotten you all mixed up. When we get to the dance, we'll have so much fun you'll be sorry you've missed out on all the others."

"I–I–"

"It's as simple as this. Do you want to be with me or don't you?"

"You know I do, Alex."

"Then it's settled. We're going to the dance."

The rest of the day dragged endlessly for Robin. She had to go to the dance even though she really didn't want to. If she didn't, Alex would never go out with her again. He'd as good as told her that. And she would just die if she lost him.

Robin had a few anxious moments the night of the dance, wondering whether or not she'd be able to get out for it. However, her parents decided to go to a concert. As soon as they were gone, she dressed frantically and left a note for her parents.

"I've gone over to Peggy's to study for some tests tomorrow," she wrote. "It may be late when I get home. Love, Robin."

She went down by the drugstore where Alex was waiting for her.

"Hi there." He smiled brightly.

She spoke to him, but that was all.

"Now, what's the trouble with you?" he asked. "Did your parents give you a bad time?"

She shook her head.

"Don't tell me your conscience is still hurting you about going to an innocent little thing like a dance?"

"I don't feel right about going," she told him, "if that's what you mean."

"Now don't act that way." He put his arm around her. "We're going to have a good time tonight, Robin. Just wait and see."

She forced a thin smile but did not reply. The muscles in her throat were tight, and she ached inside.

"Don't be a spoilsport," he said. "If you are, you're going to ruin everything. We're not doing anything wrong. We're not going to rob a bank or set fire to an old people's home or start to drink. We're just going to a good, clean dance."

She laid a hand on his arm.

"I'm sorry, Alex. I–I'll try to feel differently about it."

"If you don't, you'll ruin the evening for both of us."

When they got to the building, they went inside and took off their coats. The music was already reverberating through the high school gymnasium, and the floor was filled with kids dancing. Robin stopped uncertainly on the sidelines. She couldn't dance like that. Not out in public at least. For an instant or two she fought an all but uncontrollable desire to turn and run from the building.

Alex glanced at her but did not speak.

"There are Ellie Dwyer and Louis Baker," she said after a time, more to make conversation than anything else. "I thought they graduated last year."

"They did," Alex replied, "but the dance committee thought it would be a good idea to invite last year's class back for the dance tonight."

"Oh."

"How about it?" His voice rose. "Are we going to dance or are we going to stand here all evening?"

The corners of her mouth twitched, and her eyes reflected her obvious distaste for what she was about to do. Alex snorted his disgust.

"Aw, come on, Robin. Look as though you're having a good time whether you are or not. Everybody in the place is looking at you."

Robin produced a mechanical smile on her face and allowed him to lead her out on the floor. The music started again, and they began to dance. She had only danced a few times, but rhythm was in her body. As they began to keep time to the frantic throbbing of the drums and the blare of the trumpet, the beat seemed to take hold of her, almost against her will. She abandoned herself to the wildly exhilarating music as completely as anyone else in the big gymnasium. Excitement flushed her face, and her young heart hammered. When the music finally stopped playing several minutes later, she felt limp and breathless.

Alex eyed her admiringly.

"Now that's more like it. That was really great, wasn't it?"

Robin did not answer. She couldn't say that she had enjoyed the dance. Rather, it seemed that the music with its fascinating beat had completely taken possession of her. And the shame of doing what she knew in her heart was wrong clenched icy fingers at her throat.

"How'd you like it?" he asked.

She swallowed with difficulty and tried to sound happy.

"It was all right."

"All right?" he echoed. "It was more than all right. It was great. I'm going to tell you something, Robin. You're going to be a great little dancer as soon as you learn to let yourself go." The music started once more, and he held out his hand. "Shall we give it a whirl again?"

She shook her head.

"Let's go over and sit down for a while."

For the next two dances they sat along the sidelines, watching. She looked at her watch. The time was crawling away!

Never again! If she got through this evening, she'd never come to a thing like this anymore.

They were still sitting there when a couple of kids from Robin's English class came by. The girl stopped curiously.

"Well, hello," she said.

"Hi."

There was a brief pause. The girl stared at her. "When I looked over here a few minutes ago and saw you, I thought I must be seeing things. I had no idea you'd *ever* come to a dance." There was mockery in her voice.

Robin felt her cheeks stain crimson. This was something she hadn't counted on – the attitude of the kids. Alex got quickly to his feet.

"Come on, Robin, let's dance."

And, because she could think of no excuse for not dancing anymore, she got to her feet and followed him out on the floor. It was even worse this time than it had been before. She hoped Alex didn't notice.

She thought the evening would never wear away, but finally the time for refreshments came. Robin told Alex she was tired and wanted to leave, but he was in no hurry to go.

"Let's have something to eat before we go at least," he said. "You might not be hungry, but I am. I'm starved."

"It won't take long, will it?" she asked uneasily.

He caught the concern in her voice. "Who are you?" he asked tauntingly. "Cinderella?"

"I've got to be in early tonight, Alex," she protested lamely. "You know how Mom and Dad are. They never will let me out at night if they–they find out where I am tonight."

He nodded understandingly.

"Okay. Okay. We'll get in at the front of the line and leave as soon as we get something to eat."

For several minutes neither of them noticed whom they were standing behind. Joe Chamberlain, who had dropped out of school the year before when he was a senior, turned around and saw them.

"Alex Smith," he exclaimed. "How are you? Haven't seen you since we met last summer!"

"Joe!"

Joe's young wife, Nellie, smiled warmly at Robin.

"Hello, Robin," she said. "It's so nice to see you here." There was no mistaking what she meant. Robin felt the color come back into her face.

"Well," Alex continued, "how's married life these days?"

Joe beamed. "Great! Just great! We haven't been sorry about getting married for a minute, have we, Nellie?"

She giggled. "The only thing we've been sorry about is that we didn't quit school and get married a year ago."

When they had been served, Robin, Alex, Nellie, and Joe went to one corner of the gym and found chairs a little apart from the others.

"I've wondered how the two of you have been getting along since you quit school last year to get married," Robin said. "Have you been sorry?"

Nellie's eyes sparkled. "Sorry?" she repeated. "Why would we have been sorry? It's the most marvelous thing we ever could have done." She laid a hand on Robin's arm. "Joe and I have so much fun taking care of our apartment. He helps me clean and do the dishes, and he goes down to the laundromat with me and everything."

"You make it sound exciting."

"Oh, it is. You don't know what it is to be happy until you're married. You don't have anyone telling you what you can or can't do or anything."

Alex and Joe turned around just then.

"I've been telling Robin how happy we've been since we got married, Joe," she said.

He grinned. "You'll have to watch it, Alex. Nellie's liable to do such a good selling job with Robin that she'll be wanting to get married too."

"Worse things than that could happen."

"Why don't you kids come over sometime? I'm just dying to show you our apartment."

"Only you'd better give us a little warning so we can get it straightened up."

"We'll be up one of these nights soon," Alex said. "You've got us curious now."

Alex and Robin got their coats and left the school. She looked down at her watch.

"I've got to hurry," she exclaimed fearfully. "I think maybe I can beat my parents home tonight, and I'm going to have to or I'm going to be in real trouble."

They got into the car, and Alex started the engine.

"Know something?" There was a new, faraway tone in his voice. "Joe and Nellie really have something, don't they?"

CHAPTER 2

MR. EVANS' ULTIMATUM

Robin got home a few minutes before her parents did that evening. When they returned, she was already in bed. She pretended to be asleep when her mother opened her bedroom door and peeked in.

"Robin's home already, Richard," she said.

"That's a switch. Usually I have to wait up half the night for her."

"You've got to give her credit when she does do right, you know. We can't continually find fault with her."

Her dad frowned. "It's not hard to find fault with her the way she's been acting since we got her that car and she started going with that young Smith," he blurted. "That's for sure."

Robin, who could hear what they said, sat upright in bed. Her temper flamed. What right did they have to think such terrible things about her as that?

It didn't do any good to try and do what she ought to do. Nobody would give her credit for anything.

The following morning Robin was in such a hurry to get to school that she scarcely had time to speak to them. As it was, she feared they would be able to read the guilt in her eyes. Somehow she managed to put the dance out of her mind during the day. In fact, she didn't think of it again until she got home from school that evening. Her dad was waiting for her. His face was dark with concern.

"Robin," he said.

She stopped hesitantly. When he used that tone of voice, something was terribly wrong.

"Yes?" she said, turning slowly.

"I want to talk to you."

She went on into the living room and stood there uneasily, her gaze searching his.

"What was it you wanted, Dad?" she asked testily. "You know I've got a lot of studies to get to."

"They can wait."

She started to reply curtly but stopped. "Yes, they can wait, I suppose."

"I heard something about you today that was very disturbing to me. Very disturbing."

Color crept up in her cheeks, but her eyes flamed their defiance. "What have I done now?"

He took a deep breath. "Robin, you know what your mother and I think about dancing and that sort of thing, don't you?" In spite of his obvious effort to keep his temper, his voice rose.

"I ought to," she snapped. "You preach it often enough."

A hurt look crossed his face. She was sorry for what she had said but couldn't bring herself to apologize. She sat down across from him and waited.

"Apparently it hasn't done any good."

"I–I'm sorry, Daddy," she began. She didn't really want to hurt him, but he had no right to talk to her like that. That was one of the big troubles. Her parents wouldn't let her think for herself. They treated her as though she was a three-year-old!

Mr. Evans cleared his throat.

"Robin," he began. Then he paused and took a deep breath. "Tell me the truth. Did you go to that dance last night?"

She did not reply.

"Did you?" he repeated.

She looked up, eyes flashing. "What if I did?" she demanded angrily. "I'm old enough to know what I want to do and what I don't want to do. You and Mom can't live my life for me!"

He spoke slowly. "We don't want to live your life for you, my dear. But as long as you live here at home, you are to obey the rules of this home. And one of those rules is that you are not to dance or go to dances. Is that clear?"

She caught her breath sharply. She couldn't tell them that she had gone only because Alex wanted her to. That would only make her dad more sure than ever that Alex was a bad influence on her.

"I–I only went because you and mom make such a fuss about things like that," she said lamely. "And the kids would ask me what I had against dances, and I wouldn't know because I–I'd never gone to any. So I went just to–to see what they were like."

Mr. Evans was a long while in continuing. And when he spoke, it was almost as though he had not even heard what she said.

"What is it that's made you change this way, Robin?" he asked. "A year or so ago you only had one desire. That was to live for Christ. You were always at church activities and wouldn't have thought of sneaking out and going to a dance or anything else that we had asked you not to go to. Why are you so different now than you used to be?"

"I'm not any different than I've ever been!" she exclaimed defensively. "But all of a sudden, you've started treating me like a baby. You act as though you don't trust me or something."

Her dad went on. "The only thing I can think of that would cause you to act the way you have been acting is that you're running around with this Alex Smith character."

Tears suddenly flooded Robin's eyes and trickled down her cheeks. "Don't blame Alex for everything, Dad," she told him between sobbing. "You–you might just as well know the truth. I love Alex, and he loves me!"

Mr. Evans got slowly to his feet and towered over her. It was almost a minute before he spoke again.

"Robin," he said, "I don't want you to go out with Alex anymore."

"Daddy!" she cried. "You can't do that to me! You just can't!"

"I can and I will. If you can't go out with Alex and maintain a good Christian testimony, then it's time you quit dating him altogether. And that's final!"

Robin leaped to her feet and, shoulders twitching, she charged into her room and slammed the door so hard that the pictures on either side jumped in protest.

Mrs. Evans, who had been half listening from the kitchen, went over to her husband. "Now, what was that all about?" she asked.

"I just told Robin that she had to quit going out with that Smith kid," he said. "That's all that's wrong."

Dismay darkened her face.

"Oh, I wish you hadn't done that, Richard."

"You wish I hadn't done it?" He stared at her incredulously. "Just what do you mean by that crack? Are you in favor of letting him drag her all the way down into sin?"

"Of course not, Richard. But to make them break up! It seems so–so cruel."

"Maybe it does, but I've already done it. Robin's not going out with that kid again. And that's final!"

* * *

Over at the Orlis home Jim Morgan was still as highly critical as ever of everything that Kent Gilbert did.

"I tell you, Danny," he said, "that guy is bad medicine! We all thought it was going to help him so much to get him to go to camp, but it didn't do a bit of good! He's no different now than he was when he went there."

"We can't expect him to be any different, Jim," Danny said quietly. "He didn't accept Christ as his Savior. That's the only thing that would make a change in Him."

Jim snorted.

"I wonder if he's *ever* going to make a decision for Christ." He crossed the room and came back. "You know, Danny, he's going to get into some real trouble again one of these times."

Danny did not speak for a moment or two. But when he did, there was a strange tone in his voice.

"Jim, sit down for a minute," he said. "There's something I'd like to talk with you about."

Jim did as he was told.

"I know that Kent isn't a Christian, and I know that there are a lot of other things wrong in his life. I know that what you say about his getting into real trouble again may very well be true. He might have to get into deep trouble before he accepts the Lord. But, Jim, I think you ought to examine your attitude toward Kent."

Jim bristled slightly. "And what do you mean by that?"

"I might be wrong about this," Danny continued. "In fact, for your sake I hope that I am. But I get the feeling that you get real satisfaction when something bad happens to Kent."

"I'm just being realistic, that's all."

"Have you been praying for Kent's salvation, Jim?" Danny asked quietly.

"I–I–"

"Instead of being so critical of him, you ought to be praying for him. He needs our prayers. God is the only One who can work in his life and bring him to Himself."

Jim's face flushed white.

"I don't know what's the matter with you. You always stick up for Kent, Danny. I know what kind of a guy he is, that's all. It makes me mad to see him pull the wool over your eyes the way he does. He gets away with anything he wants to get away with around here."

Slowly Danny shook his head. "I feel sorry for you, Jim. I really feel sorry for you."

* * *

Robin stayed in her room for an hour or more, sobbing uncontrollably. At last her mother opened the door and tiptoed in.

"Robin?" she began.

There was no answer.

"Robin!"

"Leave me alone!" the girl retorted roughly.

"Honey, I want to talk to you."

"I don't want to talk to you or–or anybody." Her sobbing grew louder. "Nobody cares anything about me! Nobody cares whether I'm happy or not."

Mrs. Evans closed the door and came over to sit on the edge of the bed. She put her hand on her daughter's quivering shoulders. "Now, Robin," she went on, "don't feel so badly."

"How do you expect me to feel?" Robin sat up, her eyes blazing. "Dad treats me as though I'm a baby. He acts as though I don't even have any feelings. He seems to think that I'm not old enough to know who I want to go with or what I want to do!"

"Now, honey, Daddy doesn't want to run your life any more than I do," her mother went on. "It's just that he's been so deeply hurt by what you've done, and for that reason he's said some things that probably seem a little harsh to you."

"Do–do you know what he told me, Mom?" The girl's voice broke. "He told me that I–I can never go anywhere with Alex again."

Her mother nodded. "I know. He was just telling me about it."

"Then you wonder why I–I feel so bad."

"Does Alex really mean that much to you, sweetheart?"

Their eyes met.

"Oh, Mom!"

"There. There." Mrs. Evans patted the sobbing girl on the shoulder. "Everything's going to be all right."

"I don't know how you can say that. Dad has practically ruined my whole life!"

"There now, Robin," she said. "Don't feel so bad. I'll talk to Dad. I'm sure that he doesn't want to hurt you. All he wants for you is to have the very best of the Lord's will for your life."

There was a brief silence.

"Dad doesn't care about me," she went on tearfully. "He just wants to be mean!"

"That's not true, Robin. He loves you very much. You know that." Mrs. Evans hugged her close. "I'll talk to Dad after he's had time to cool off a little. I'll work things out for you!"

Robin dried her eyes.

"You–you will?" she echoed, doubt creeping into her voice. "Do you really mean it, Mom?"

"Of course I mean it." Her smile was warm and conciliatory. "I'll talk to him. And I'm sure that when he has had time to think about it, he'll realize that he was a little hasty with his decision."

Robin caught her breath.

"Oh, Mom! You don't know what this means to me! If you can get Dad to change his mind, I–I'll–"

"He'll change his mind," she promised softly. "You'll see."

Mrs. Evans left her daughter and went back into

the living room where her husband was sitting reading a book.

"How is she, Gladys?" he asked.

"I think she feels a little better."

There was a brief silence.

"I suppose she thinks I'm the meanest father in the world."

Gladys smiled. "Well, maybe you were a little hard on her."

"Hard on her?" His voice crescendoed. "Do you realize that she has deliberately defied us?"

She nodded.

"But it's not Robin who's causing the trouble," he went on. "I'm convinced of that now since this dance episode. I'm sure that it's that Smith kid she's been running around with." He breathed deeply. "But she won't be seeing him anymore. That's for certain."

He put his book down thoughtfully. For a moment or so his wife studied the concern in his face.

"Don't you think you're making a mistake in laying down an ultimatum like that, Richard?" she asked.

His eyes flashed.

"No, I don't think I'm making a mistake in laying down an ultimatum like that." His frown deepened. "I don't know what you think, Gladys, but we've got to put a stop to this while we still can. I've been thinking and thinking about it all day today. I'm convinced the trouble is this Alex Smith and that our troubles with Robin will be over when we get rid of him. So, that's what I did. I told her that he isn't welcome around here anymore. She's not to date him or even to walk home from school with him. I don't even want her to talk to him in the halls."

"But, Richard," his wife protested, "I told Robin that–"

"I don't care what you told her!" he broke in angrily. "I said that she's not going out with Alex Smith anymore and that's exactly what I mean!"

CHAPTER 3

ALEX POPS THE QUESTION

The next morning Robin waited in her room, pretending to be doing her hair and studying, until her father went to work. Then she hurried to the kitchen and asked her mother about the talk she had with him.

"Did you get to talk to Dad?" she asked. Excitement edged her voice.

Gladys nodded.

"I talked with him."

The girl read the answer in her mother's eyes.

"He still said I'd have to stop seeing Alex, didn't he?" she asked.

Her mother did not answer her directly. "He was still angry, Robin."

Robin's temper flared. "I knew it!" she exploded. "He just acts that way because he knows that I love Alex. That's why he wants to put the blame on him for everything that's happened. That's why he wants to break us up! He just doesn't want me to have any fun, that's all."

Mrs. Evans was careful in what she said. "That's not it at all," she began. "Dad just wants what is best for his little girl."

Robin's eyes flashed angrily.

"If he wanted what's best for me, would he try to make me lose the only person I–I've ever loved?"

Mrs. Evans patted her on the shoulder tenderly.

"Don't be so upset, my dear," she said quietly. "I'm sure he'll change his mind when he stops to think about the way he's hurt you."

Robin laid a hand on her mother's arm. "Do–do you really think so?"

"Would I tell you that if I didn't?"

"Mom, if anything happens to break up Alex and me, I–I'll just die!"

There was a short silence.

"Nothing is going to happen to break up you two, Robin." She paused and a smile toyed with the corners of her mouth. "I don't think you realize how much Dad and I think of Alex. Dad has said more than once that Alex is one of the nicest boys you've ever gone with. He's really very fond of him."

Robin's mouth drooped into a pout.

"That isn't what he told me last night. He–he said some terrible things about Alex. I've never been hurt so–so badly in my whole life."

"Dad only said what he did because he feels that your testimony isn't what it should be, Robin," her mother went on. "When he looks back, he thinks he can see that the trouble started when you began to go out with Alex. So he blames him. If you two wouldn't do those things we feel are so questionable, I'm sure Dad wouldn't have any objections about your dating Alex."

Tears came to Robin's eyes.

"Did–did you say that you are going to talk to him about Alex for me?" she asked hopefully.

"I'll talk with him in a few days."

"But what'll I do if he asks me for a date now?" Her lips were trembling. "I–I don't really want to disobey Dad, but I don't want to lose Alex either."

Her mother smiled reassuringly.

"Just explain to Alex that everything will be all right in a few days," she said. "That will give me a little time to talk with your father again."

Robin went to school that morning and headed directly for her homeroom. Ordinarily she would have stopped in the hall to talk with Alex for a moment or two but not today. After what had happened at home last night, she didn't want to see anyone. And she especially didn't want to see Alex.

However, Alex wanted to see her. He caught up with her between classes.

"Hi." he said. "Where've you been?"

She tried to hide the concern in her eyes. "Around."

"Don't forget tonight," he told her.

Her eyes widened. "Tonight? What's going on tonight?"

"Don't you remember? We're going over to see Joe and Nellie Chamberlain."

She hesitated uneasily.

"But–" What about her dad? He had forbidden her to go out with Alex anymore.

Alex moved closer to her and lowered his voice. "Is there something wrong?" he whispered.

"Not exactly." She took a long breath, and for an instant avoided his searching gaze. "Dad just found out that I went to the dance with you. That's all."

Alex laughed. "Oh, is that all? I thought for a minute that it was something serious."

"You don't understand, Alex." Tears flooded her eyes. "He–he told me that I–I'm not to go out with you anymore. I'm not supposed to have another date with you *ever*."

"Don't let that upset you so much," he said.

She gasped. "Don't you *care*?"

"Sure, I care. But it'll blow over as soon as he cools off a little. I've been through these things before with my parents. They storm around, and I listen to them. But I don't let it keep me from doing what I please."

"But I won't be able to go with you tonight," she protested.

"Sure you will."

"But Dad said–"

"Just tell him that you're going over to some girl-friend's to study," he went on. "Your dad won't say anything to you about that."

Robin frowned. "Maybe he wouldn't, but I don't want to lie to him."

"You won't be lying. Go over to this friend's of yours. I'll pick you up over there. Then, if he asks if you went to see her, you can tell him the truth."

"Not the whole truth," she reminded him.

"For crying out loud!" he exploded. "What can your dad expect when he tries to dictate every move you make? We've got our own lives to live, Robin. We can't let him ruin everything for us. I don't care if he is your dad."

She nodded reluctantly.

"Then you'll go with me over to Joe's tonight?" he urged.

"Maybe."

"What do you mean, maybe? Are you going, or aren't you?"

"I suppose I could go tonight, but I'll have to get home early, Alex."

"Don't worry. You'll be home early. That I'll promise you."

Robin's uneasiness grew as the time approached when she would have to talk to her dad about going over to Evelyn's. She waited until they were through eating that evening.

"Would it be all right with you if I go over to Evelyn's to study for a while tonight?" she asked.

"Are you sure it's Evelyn's that you want to go to?" Doubt tinged his voice.

Robin's face clouded. "I–I don't know what I'm going to have to do to get you to believe me anymore."

"Just tell me the truth, Robin," he answered. "That's all I ask."

Anger flashed in her eyes, but her voice was quite calm. "May I go over to Evelyn's?"

"If you're sure that's where you're really going, yes. You may go to Evelyn's. But I want to be sure that you go there and not out to see this Smith kid."

She went into the bedroom without answering him and came out a few moments later with her coat and a large armload of books. Mr. Evans came over to her.

"I'm sorry I questioned you the way I did, Robin," he said, putting an arm affectionately around her shoulders.

She cringed inwardly at his touch. As soon as she could, she left the house. She drove straight to Evelyn's and studied until a little after 8:00 when Alex stopped by for her.

"I've got to run now, Evelyn," she said. "Thanks loads. I'll see you tomorrow."

She went out into the cold night air with Alex.

"Well," he said, opening the car door and helping her get into the car, "how'd it go?"

"Let's talk about something pleasant," she retorted. He started the engine and pulled slowly away from the curb. "I've never been so humiliated in all my life, Alex." Her lips trembled. "Dad treats me like a two-year-old."

Alex laughed.

"That's nothing new, is it? Haven't they been treating you like a baby all the time?"

"Yes, but it wasn't so obvious."

"We'll have to get married," he said. "Then your dad couldn't tell you what to do. He wouldn't be able to say a word."

Her eyes widened, and she caught her breath.

"Oh, I wouldn't dare. If I did, Dad would just die!"

"We ought to do it anyway," he told her. "My parents wouldn't be happy about it either. But they'd get over it as soon as they found out that it wasn't going to do them any good to yell at us."

"It might be all right," she said, doubt and hesitation rising in her voice, "but I don't know whether we should do something like that or not."

When they finally got to the Chamberlain apartment, Joe came to the door.

"Hi," he said. "We'd just about given you up. Come on in."

Alex grinned at Robin.

"To tell you the truth, we'd have been here sooner. But Robin ran into a little parent trouble at home." The young couple nodded sympathetically.

"We used to have that kind of trouble all the time," Nellie told them. "But when we got married, our parents found out that we were a lot older and more grown up than they had ever thought we were."

That evening was the most wonderful that Robin

and Alex had ever spent together. They played Monopoly with Joe and Nellie for over an hour, talking all the while about what the young couple did with their time and how happy they were now that they were married. When the time came to eat, Nellie took Robin Evans out to the kitchen with her.

"Tell me something, Nellie," Robin began seriously. "Are you and Joe always as happy as you seem to be tonight?"

A strange look came into the other girl's face, and it was a moment or two before she could answer. "Of course we are. It's just wonderful being married when you're as much in love as Joe and I are." She paused. "And I think you and Alex feel the same way about each other as we do."

"That's right." Robin's eyes softened. "When I think about the fact that I–I might have to give up Alex, I know that life wouldn't even be worth living."

"I told Joe you and Alex were that way about each other." Excitement gleamed in Nellie's eyes. "On the way home from the dance the other night I told him that I wouldn't be surprised if you two quit school and got married."

"Oh, I'd never dare do that," Robin said. "My parents would – I don't know what they would do if we quit school and got married. I think they want to keep me as their baby all of their lives."

"My parents did the same thing. You know, Robin, Joe and I wouldn't be married yet if we hadn't run away and done it on our own."

There was a brief hesitation.

"What did your parents say when you told them about it?"

Nellie laughed. "You never saw anyone so mad – for a little while. But what could they do? We were married. They couldn't change that. At least they decided not to try to change it."

"Did they ever forgive you?"

"Oh, sure. They stormed around a little, but it wasn't too long until they came around. I think they were relieved that they didn't have to try to run my life for me."

They ate about 9:30. When they finished eating, Nellie and Joe followed them down to the car.

"Thank you for a lovely evening," Robin said.

"Think over what I told you," Nellie answered.

"Oh, I will."

Getting married was an exciting thing to talk about. Alex started the engine, and they drove toward his home. Each was thinking about what had been said at the Chamberlain apartment.

"Well, Robin," he said at last. "Did you have a good time? It sort of makes you realize that Nellie and Joe have something we don't have, doesn't it?" he asked.

Robin's eyes lighted. "Oh, Alex, I can hardly wait until you and I get a place like that for ourselves." He stopped in front of his house and sat there for a moment, talking.

"You know, Robin," he continued, "you said something a minute ago about not wanting to wait until we get a place for ourselves. We don't have to wait if we don't want to."

She eyed him uneasily. "What do you mean by that?"

"We can go ahead and get married. That's what Nellie and Joe did. They didn't let *anybody* stop them."

She gasped. "Oh, Alex! I couldn't!"

Hurt came to his face. "You don't mean you couldn't. You mean that you don't want to."

"That's not it at all," she protested, putting a hand tenderly on his arm. "I want to marry you more than I want anything else in the world."

"You certainly don't sound like it."

"I do. Honestly I do. But–"

"But, what?"

"I just know what my parents would say if we got married. It would hurt them terribly."

Alex bristled.

"Robin, if you really mean what you say about loving me, you wouldn't care what they'd say."

She stared at him miserably.

"Alex," she said, "don't be like that!"

"I don't know how you can expect me to be any other way. If you really love me, Robin, you'll want to get married right now. You won't want to wait." There was a long hesitation.

"I–I–" Her voice choked.

Alex spoke softly.

"Think about it tonight, will you, Robin?" he asked tenderly. "We'll talk about it again tomorrow."

CHAPTER 4

ROBIN SURPRISES ALEX

When Robin got home that night she intended to go directly to her room, but, as usual, her dad stopped her.

"You stayed out a little late again this evening, didn't you, Robin?" he asked. He spoke quietly enough, but she thought she detected suspicion in his voice.

She turned to face him.

"It isn't even 11:00 yet, Dad. It's not late."

"I know, but you have school tomorrow."

"I don't know why you would expect me to go to bed so early." Defiance flamed in her eyes. "After all, I'm a senior in high school, you know."

He nodded.

"I just wish you'd come in a little earlier on school nights, that's all."

Briefly her temper flared. It was no wonder she didn't want to be at home, she reasoned. Whenever she and her dad were there, they were having trouble. But she did not reply to him. The evening with Alex and their young married friends had been too wonderful to ruin by getting angry. Not this night! She wanted to remember each glorious moment for always.

Always! She turned the word over in her mind. That was a song they sometimes sang at weddings. She had never liked it very well before this instant. Yet it mirrored exactly how she felt about Alex. She wanted to love him and be with him for always – forever and ever.

Robin went into her room as soon as she could and closed the door behind her. For a long while she sat at the dressing table in the dark.

Alex loved her! He actually wanted her to marry him! And she loved him more than anything else in the world. Slowly she got to her feet and walked to the window where she stood for a long while looking out. She couldn't even stand to think what life would be like without him.

"Mrs. Alex Smith!" She whispered the name softly, caressingly. She had never dreamed that anything so wonderful would happen to her when she first started going out with him.

After a time, the smile faded from her lips. It would all be so wonderful, if only her parents would try to understand that she and Alex were different than the others. If only they would realize that she and Alex were in love and couldn't stand to live apart.

It wasn't that she didn't love her parents. She loved them as much as she ever did. And pain wrenched at her heart whenever she and her dad had an argument. But there were times when he acted as though he didn't care anything at all about her, as though all he wanted to do was to make her do the things he wanted her to do.

Robin went back to the stand, switched on the bed lamp, and picked up her Bible. It was strange that she should think about reading it now. She hadn't read it for some time. But now she felt compelled to read it. For a long while she read, her hunger for the Bible growing as she did so. Finally she knelt beside the bed and began to pray.

"Dear Lord, You know I love Alex so much," she began. "I–I just can't live without him, so please make it all right with Mom and Dad for me to marry him."

Later that night, as she tried to sleep, her mind churned. But by the time she got up the next morning she had decided what she was going to do. She loved Alex and she thought that he loved her, but neither of them were through school. She couldn't marry him now before they graduated. That was all there was to it. As much as it would hurt her, she wasn't going to get married for a while. She would probably even wait until her dad and mom gave their permission, as much as that would hurt her.

She almost asked them about it at the breakfast table that morning. But her dad was reading the news and her mother had a headache. Once or twice she started to speak, but neither one of them was paying any attention to her. She decided to wait until that night when they were together around the table. She'd do it then.

When she entered the school building that morning Alex was waiting for her. As soon as he saw her, he came over to her and looked at her possessively.

"Hi, sweetheart."

Her smile was infectious. "Hi."

"Did you do any thinking about what we were talking about last night?" he whispered.

She nodded. "A–a little.

"I hardly slept at all." He drew her off to one side. "Listen. I did a little checking around this morning. I found out that we've got to have blood tests ahead of time if we're going to be married here in Minnesota. That means we're going to have to go somewhere this Saturday and get them taken."

Her forehead wrinkled uneasily. "But Alex–"

"I know how you feel," he said. "I feel the same way. But after all, we have our own lives to live. We can't let our parents decide everything for us."

"They would never forgive me," she countered. "I–I'm afraid they'd disown me if–if we went ahead and got married."

"You heard what Joe and Nellie said, didn't you."

"They had plenty of trouble. She told me about it."

"They had a little trouble, all right. I know we'd get that. But it wasn't long until their parents got over it. Ours would be the same."

"Not Dad," she said. "Mom might understand, but he would never forgive me. And I–I love him, Alex, in spite of the way he treats me. And I don't want to hurt him."

A new, insistent tone edged his voice thinly. "I don't want to hurt my parents either, Robin," he said. "But if they would let us do the way we want to, they wouldn't get hurt. Besides, they'll get over it. It's the only way."

"Maybe if we went to them together," she said, "and–and told them how much we love each other, it would make a big difference. Maybe they'd give their consent for us to be married."

Alex shook his head vigorously.

"You don't know your parents very well if you think it would. I'll bet if your dad had his way, he'd make us wait 'til we were forty before he'd let us get married."

Robin looked about quickly to see if anyone had heard him.

"Alex," she said, "don't talk so loud. If anyone hears us, we'll really be in trouble."

His voice lowered again.

"Okay," he said, "but I'm not ashamed of the way I feel about you. I want everyone to know that I love you and that I want to marry you."

"Not now," she protested. "Not yet. I don't want anyone to know!"

He took a deep breath.

"All right, have it your way. What time Saturday do you want to go for those blood tests?"

"I–I don't know," she said reluctantly. "I'll have to–to think about it and–and talk to you about it later."

"There's nothing to talk about. All we've got to do is decide whether we're going in the morning or the afternoon."

"I'll see you after school. Okay?"

"Okay. I'll meet you here by the door."

Miserably Robin went to class. She should have told Alex that she couldn't marry him now. That she had decided she wasn't going to marry him until her parents gave their consent. But how could she do it? How could she make him understand without running the risk of losing him?

When classes were over that afternoon, Alex was standing at the door.

"I just thought of something," he said in guarded tones. "The doctor's offices might be closed Saturday afternoon. We'll have to skip school tomorrow and take care of it then. I'll meet you at the drugstore at 9:30."

She swallowed hard.

"I can't go then. The principal's office might call the house to see if I was sick and we'd be in big trouble."

"Hmmm." He pursed his lips. "You might be right, at that. I'll find out if the doctor's offices aren't open for a little while Saturday morning. If they are, we can take care of it then. If they aren't, we'll just have to run the risk of skipping school."

Several times during the rest of the week Robin resolved to tell Alex that she had to back out – that, regardless of how much she loved him, she couldn't go through with it. But each time the words choked in her throat.

Alex learned that the doctor's offices were open Saturday morning, and the next Saturday they met at the drugstore about 9:30.

"Well, how did it go for you, Robin?" Alex asked as they walked to the car together.

"I had a terrible time getting away from the house this morning," she said. "I thought Dad would never go to the office. It seemed that all he wanted to do was sit at the breakfast table and talk."

Alex laughed nervously.

"That's something we won't have to worry about much longer."

She eyed him curiously.

"After we're married, we aren't going to have to worry about what other people do or think or say. We'll be strictly on our own."

She smiled weakly but said nothing.

They drove to a clinic in a nearby town and went in to have their blood tests. Robin hesitated.

"Come on, Robin," Alex urged. "This isn't anything. All they do is take a little blood out of each of us. It won't take more than a couple of minutes."

"But–"

"Don't worry. I'll do the talking."

With great reluctance she followed him inside the building.

What he said was true. It wasn't difficult, nor was it as embarrassing as she had thought it would be. They went into the doctor's office, a technician came in and got a sample of blood, and they were on their way back to the car.

"See," Alex said, "that wasn't so bad, was it?"

"No. I–I thought it would be worse."

"Well, we'd better be getting back home so your parents won't get suspicious and start asking a lot of stupid questions. We don't want anything happening now that might ruin things."

Robin leaned back in the seat and for a moment or two closed her eyes. A feeling of excitement filled her entire body. She was going to be married! Kay had tried to tell her once that being a missionary was the most important thing in all the world. But right now, she knew that there was nothing any more important than her happiness with Alex.

* * *

As long as Robin and Alex had been dating, they had been together almost every Sunday night. But on this particular Sunday evening, her dad insisted that she go to church with her mother and him.

"I'd like to, Daddy," she said lamely, "but–but I've got some studying to do."

"The service only lasts an hour. You'll have plenty of time to study when we get home."

"But we're having tests tomorrow," she protested.

He still did not relent. "Robin, you are going to church with us tonight. Is that clear?"

There was no way she could get out of it. No way at all. The first chance she had she called Alex and told him that she wouldn't be able to go with him that night. He seemed singularly undisturbed.

"That's okay," he said. "Then we won't have to worry about your dad's getting wind of you know what."

Even though she was talking over the phone, her cheeks colored slightly.

"I want to go out with you tonight," she said. "I'll just be miserable sitting in church when I know I could be out with you. But he won't listen to me."

"Don't get so upset about it. I think it's great. Then he'll be sure that we're not seeing each other anymore."

Thoughtfully she hung up and went to her room to get ready for church. It was true that her dad had forbidden her to go out with Alex. In spite of her mother's efforts, he had not changed his mind.

At church that night the pastor preached a strong message on dedicating our lives to God. At first Robin thought that her father must have known about the subject and that was the reason he had insisted that she go to church that night. Her temper flared briefly. Then she realized that he couldn't have known. The pastor said he wasn't bringing the message he had planned to bring.

"It is not enough for us to accept Christ as our Savior," he said. "We must make Him the Lord and Master of our lives. We must yield fully and completely to Him."

Robin Evans heard everything the pastor was saying, but at the same time her mind began to wander. There was a time when all she thought about was Bible club and the kids at school who needed to accept Christ. Her one desire was to serve Christ in the very best way she knew how.

She remembered vividly her concern about going out as a missionary. There had been a time – it seemed ages ago – when she felt that what God wanted her to do was the most important thing in all the world. But all of that seemed to be so long ago. Now there was Alex, and he was the most important thing in her life. She wondered how she could ever have been concerned about anything else.

At last the message was over and the pastor was giving the invitation.

"If there is anyone here who wants to live for Christ in a way you have never lived for Him before," he concluded, "I am going to ask you to come down to the front of the church while we sing a closing hymn. Those of you who want to live differently than you are living today – who want your lives never to be the same again – won't you come forward now?"

The invitation went on a little longer, but Robin steeled herself against it. She wanted to go forward and get some of the things in her life settled again.

She wanted to have the old relationship with the Lord reestablished. She wanted it desperately. But if she yielded to the Lord, it would mean that she would lose Alex. And she couldn't do that. Her life wouldn't be worth living without him!

* * *

That night Robin Evans tossed restlessly in her bed until almost midnight. Now and then she prayed, or tried to as the questions raced, unanswered, through her mind. Before she dropped off to sleep, however, she knew what she had to do.

* * *

The next morning, she made a point to see Alex before class.

"Alex," she said, her voice choked. "I've got to talk to you."

Fear leaped to his eyes.

"What's the matter?"

"I've just got to tell you something." She fought desperately to control the tremor in her voice.

"What do you mean?"

"Alex, I–I can't date you anymore." Anguish flickered in her eyes. "I can't marry you unless you become a Christian. I just can't!"

CHAPTER 5

A WRONG MOVE

Alex stared at Robin, his eyes widening incredulously.

"What are you talking about?" His voice grew louder. "Are you out of your mind or something?"

"I know it sounds silly to you, Alex, but last night at church our pastor preached a message that really got to me. I'm afraid I haven't been a very good Christian."

"That's stupid," he exclaimed.

"Let me finish." There was desperation in her voice. "I had a terrible battle with myself before I–I finally came to a decision. But I've made it now, Alex, and I know it's the right one. I–I can't marry you. I don't even have the right to go out with you unless you become a Christian."

There! It was out! She waited breathlessly.

Alex's handsome young face flushed, and anger narrowed his eyes.

"You mean you want to break up?" he demanded. "Is that it? What's the deal? Have you gotten tired of going out with me?"

"No, that isn't it at all! You know I don't want to break up with you. I–I don't know how I could stand it if we did break up!"

"Then forget it!"

"But I know that I shouldn't marry a person who isn't a Christian."

For the space of half a minute Alex's gaze bore into hers.

"Is that the only thing this is all about?" he asked seriously. "You're sure this isn't some kind of an excuse?"

"Alex!" She was close to tears. "You know it isn't an excuse. I can hardly stand it when I think of–of losing you."

He laid his hand on her arm reassuringly.

"Then don't give it another thought."

"But–but–"

"I told you that I'll go to church with you as soon as you're my wife. I give you my word on it."

"But that's not the point, Alex," she countered. "You need to become a Christian. The Bible says–"

He broke in quickly. "Look, Robin, I might take you up on that Christian bit one of these days, but I don't like the idea of having you try to blackmail me into it.

"I–I–you're taking me all wrong," she said. "That isn't what I meant at all."

"Then let's not talk about it anymore." He lowered his voice. "You and I have a lot of plans to make. Those blood tests ought to be back today or tomorrow. Anytime after that–" He winked at her knowingly.

Robin was even more disturbed than before as she went to her homeroom. This wasn't the way she had planned it at all. She had thought she would be able to convince Alex that he ought to take a stand for the Lord Jesus Christ. After all, he knew that she was a Christian and he loved her a great deal. She had thought he would want to accept Christ simply because she wanted him to. But he hadn't. The ache in her heart continued to grow.

* * *

Robin wasn't the only one who was deeply touched by the Sunday night message. Jim Morgan had been stirred too. The way he had treated Kent drove barbs deeply into his heart.

He had not gone forward that night either. But at home, after everyone else had gone to bed, he knelt and prayed for forgiveness.

He had planned on talking to Kent the next morning, but he had to be at school early and Kent had chosen that day to oversleep. So it wasn't until after school that Jim got to talk to him. He got home early and was waiting in the living room when Kent came in.

"Now, what's on your mind?" Kent asked.

"I'd like to talk to you."

"For cryin' out loud, can't a guy come home without havin' somebody jump on him."

Jim ignored the edge to Kent's voice. "I want to tell you that after hearing the message at church last night I realized that I haven't had the right attitude toward you. I've been stubborn and over critical and I–I'm sorry."

A sneer marred Kent's youthful face. "You ain't tellin' me nothin'."

"Will–will you forgive me?"

Kent sneered. "What're you tryin' to do? Get in good with Danny and Kay or something?"

"I'm apologizing for the way I've been acting toward you. That's all."

"You might fool somebody, but you ain't foolin' me none. You don't really mean what you're saying. You've got some sort of an angle. Come on. What is it?"

"There isn't any angle. I just want you to know that I'm sorry for the way I've treated you. I want to get things straightened out with you so–so I can get my life straightened out with the Lord."

Kent laughed.

"I don't know whether I'll forgive you or not," he said. "I suppose it all depends on how you treat me from now on."

Jim clenched his fists momentarily and his temper flared. What was the matter with Kent anyway?

Then he relaxed and forced a thin smile to his lips. It didn't make any difference how Kent treated him. The thing that was important was that he treat Kent the way a Christian should.

* * *

School hadn't gone at all well for Robin that day. And when she came home that night, she was still rather disturbed. After a short time, her dad came in.

Robin saw that there was something wrong the instant he opened the door. He stopped and looked down at her angrily.

"Robin," he exclaimed, "I thought I told you that I didn't want you to go out with Alex Smith anymore!"

Her face blanched, but she made no reply.

"Well, didn't I?"

"I haven't been dating him, Daddy."

"Now, Robin, don't lie to me. When I went to the office this morning, I was only half a block behind you. You stopped in front of the drugstore and picked up that young hoodlum!"

"Daddy!" The word exploded from her lips. "Alex Smith is not a hoodlum! You can't say things like that about him!"

"You were with Alex after I had forbidden you to go out with him."

"But we didn't have a date. I just took him to school, that's all. I don't think that's such a terrible crime."

His expression changed. "Robin, I don't know what has happened to you these last few months. I confess I can't understand it at all. You aren't the same girl you used to be."

Her eyes flashed her defiance. "I'm the same person I've always been!" Tears trembled in her voice. "The only thing wrong is that you treat me like a baby."

"If you're going to act like a baby, I'm going to treat you like one!" he snapped. A moment later he lowered his voice. "I can't have you disobeying me, Robin." He took a deep breath and his anger flashed again. "For the next thirty days you are not to go anywhere with anyone except your mother and me. Is that clear?"

Helplessly she stared up at him. For an instant it appeared as though she was about to speak but checked herself. She was crying now silently.

"If–if you're going to treat me that way, I'd just as well be dead!" She dashed into the bedroom, slammed the door behind her, and threw herself onto the bed.

Mrs. Evans stood by helplessly.

"I do wish you would be a little more tolerant and understanding when you're dealing with Robin, Richard," she said. "She's going through a very difficult time of her life. She needs a little patience in the way she's handled."

He sat down wearily and crossed his legs. "It takes more than patience, tolerance, and understanding," he said. "It takes firmness right now. Do you realize, Gladys, that she deliberately disobeyed us."

Mrs. Evans sat down across from him. "But she didn't really date this boy. You've got to admit that."

"As far as we know," he added, "She was with him after I told her that she couldn't go out with him again. I don't know what you can call it except disobedience."

"Don't you think we're being a little hard on her insisting that she give up Alex?" she asked. "After all, he is a nice boy from a good family."

Mr. Evans scowled deeply.

"He may be from a good family and all of that, but that boy isn't a Christian and he's not good for Robin. Ever since she started going out with him, she's done things she never thought of doing before."

Mrs. Evans stood and went slowly into the kitchen without saying any more. At the supper table that evening, the conversation was strained and unnatural.

* * *

The following Friday evening Mr. and Mrs. Evans attended an adult Bible study class. Before they left the house, however, Robin's dad looked in on her.

"I want to remind you that you're not to go anywhere tonight, Robin."

She looked up at him.

"Where would I go? You've forbidden me to be with any of my friends."

He hesitated as though he had something more to say but turned on his heel and left.

They went to the Bible study and got home shortly before 10:00.

"It was a nice study, wasn't it?" Mrs. Evans asked.

Her husband nodded. "I wonder if Robin is here or if she's sneaked out."

"Of course she'll be home. She told you she would be, didn't she?"

"She's told me a lot of things lately that haven't proved to be true."

He drove into the garage, and they walked into the house together.

"Robin," he called out, "we're home."

There was no answer.

"Robin?" Mr. Evans' voice raised. He strode forward and knocked on her door.

"Don't make so much noise, dear," his wife cautioned. "She may be asleep."

For answer, he pushed open the bedroom door and switched on the light. His body stiffened.

"She's not here!"

Incredulously, they stared at one another. It was a moment or two before either could speak.

"Do you realize that Robin has gone out again after she told us that she was going to stay home tonight?"

"Maybe she had to go to the library."

"At this hour?" he echoed.

"She might have gone over to Evelyn's house to study."

"Or she might have gone out riding with that Smith kid again," he said. His voice crescendoed.

Gladys laid a hand on her husband's arm. Richard, don't get so worked up until we find out where she is. She probably has a perfectly good reason for being gone."

He paced across the floor to the window where he stood looking up the deserted, snow-packed street. Then he came back to where his wife was standing, anguish lining his face.

"I don't know what we're going to do with her, Gladys. Sometimes I think she'll be the death of both of us."

"I'm as concerned about her as you are," his wife said, "but I have confidence in our little girl that she'll get straightened out before long and be the same sweet little daughter she's always been."

"I don't see how you can say that when there's been one act of defiance against another. She's getting more undependable all the time."

"I'll never forget how I acted when I got my first boyfriend," his wife continued, a faraway look in her eyes. "It was the most wonderful, confusing time of my life."

There was a long silence.

"I'm tired, Richard," she said at last. "I think I'm going to bed."

"You go ahead. I'm going to wait up until Robin comes home. I want to have a little talk with her tonight."

Questions flickered uncertainly in his wife's eyes.

"All right," she said, "but when you talk to her, just don't forget that you were young once."

Without replying, he dropped to a big reclining chair and eyed the clock. A thousand questions raced unanswered through his mind. Robin had always been such a dependable girl with a radiant Christian testimony. What had gone wrong?

Come to think of it, he mused, this trouble started about the time he gave her that car. He sat up straight. That was what he would do! He'd take the car away from her. Not for good but maybe for a week or two. That ought to make her realize things were going to have to change. The car was her most prized possession. Just the thought that she might lose it ought to be enough to bring her to her senses.

Carefully he planned what he would say.

"Young lady, you've stayed out past your curfew for the last time. I want the keys to your car."

He could hear her protests. They would be tearful and prolonged, but this was one time they weren't going to work. It didn't make any difference what Robin or Gladys said. He wasn't going to weaken.

"And what's more, if you don't straighten up, I'm going to take it to the garage and sell it. And while we're on the subject, if I catch you with that Smith kid again, you'll never drive that red convertible again. So you'll have to make a choice."

That would do it! She would give up most anything for that car.

Impatiently he looked at the clock. Robin really should be in by this time. It was almost 11:00.

Uneasily he went to the window to look out again. After a while he went back to the chair and leaned back, closing his eyes.

He must have dozed. He didn't hear the clock strike 12:00 or 12:30. When he finally stirred restlessly and noticed the time, it was almost 1:00.

Icy fingers of fear grasped his lungs and squeezed them relentlessly until he could scarcely breathe. He went to the door to Robin's room and looked in, but she was not there.

"Gladys!" he exclaimed. "Gladys!"

His wife mumbled unintelligibly.

"Gladys! Robin isn't in yet."

Instantly Mrs. Evans was awake.

"Are you sure?" she demanded. For the first time fear crept into her voice.

"Of course I'm sure! She's not here. I tell you, something must have happened to her!"

Gladys Evans got out of bed and slipped into a robe. When she came out into the living room, her face was ashen.

"What are we going to do?" she asked.

"I'm going to phone the Smiths and find out if Alex is there or if he knows where she went tonight."

His hands were shaking so much he could scarcely dial the number.

CHAPTER 6

TWO FAMILIES WAIT

Earlier that evening Robin had hurriedly packed her suitcase and dressed in her new blue taffeta dress. She was glad that her mom and dad were attending the Friday night Bible study, for both she and Alex felt it was best to leave quietly and not have to create another scene. She took a final glance in the mirror. The corsage would look lovely on this dress.

Alex stopped by a few minutes before 8:00 and they picked up Joe and Nellie Chamberlain before heading out of town.

"Are you excited, Robin?" Alex asked, a smile in his voice.

"Sort of." The corners of her mouth tightened. She was excited and a little afraid too. "Did you leave a note for your parents?"

"Nope. They'll find out soon enough."

Robin thought for a moment.

"I knew how Mom and Dad would worry," she said, "so I left a note explaining that we're eloping and that we'd see them after the honeymoon."

"For crying out loud! That's taking quite a chance. If they find out too soon, they're apt to take out after us and catch us before we have a chance to get married."

She shook her head.

"I put it under the mirror on the dresser. They won't find it for quite a while, so don't worry."

Nellie and Joe had said very little up to this point, but Nellie finally spoke up. "I think you were right, Robin. After we got married, I sort of wished I had left a note. My mother was terribly worried that I'd been in an accident or killed or something."

"Yeah," Joe said, "but if they'd caught us, we never would have been able to get married."

Robin leaned back and closed her eyes. This hadn't been the way she wanted to get married. She had always dreamed of a church wedding with her closest friend as maid of honor and with the church decorated with scads of flowers. She had always wanted her father to walk down the aisle with her and give her away.

It was her parents' fault that she couldn't be married that way. They were so stubborn they didn't even want her to go out with Alex, let alone marry him. She didn't have any choice. Not unless she wanted to risk losing him altogether. And she would die if that happened. She would just die.

At the next town Alex pulled up before a truck stop, service station, and cafe.

"Want to come in with me?" he asked grinning.

"Wh-what are you going to do?"

"Find out where the nearest preacher lives."

She shook her head. "I–I'll wait out here with Nellie and Joe."

In a few moments he was back.

"We're in luck, sweetheart." He started the engine and edged back onto the highway. "There's a justice of the peace who lives in the last house on the other side of town."

"Oh, Alex!" Dismay edged her voice. "I don't want to be married by a justice of the peace. I want to be married by a minister."

He shrugged his shoulders.

"Sorry. The preacher of the only church in town is away at some sort of a conference. He won't be back until Sunday."

Dismay grew in Robin's heart.

"It doesn't make any difference who marries us," he told her. "They use the same words. It all means the same."

"I know, but–" She swallowed hard.

They turned into the driveway of the place where they had been directed and stopped. The house was dark.

"They must be in bed," Alex mumbled to himself.

"You can soon find out about that," Joe told him. "Go knock on the door."

Alex went up to the front door and knocked timidly. There was no answer. He knocked again and waited, shifting nervously from one foot to the other.

Robin put down the car window and called to him. "I–I don't think there's anyone at home."

"He's home, all right." Desperation edged Alex's voice. "He's got to be home!"

Again Alex knocked. This time louder than before. Even as he did so, a car turned in at the driveway. It stopped near Robin's convertible and an angular man in a heavy topcoat got out.

"Hello there," he said.

"H-h-hello." Alex started over to him.

"I saw the car in the driveway, and I thought maybe the highway patrol had stopped here with an out-of-state speeder."

Alex laughed self-consciously. "Oh, no. We–we'd like to be married."

The tall man turned back to his car.

"Hannah," he said, "take these young people inside where it's warm. I'll put the car in the garage."

A short, graying woman got out and started for the house.

"It's a good thing Willis and I drove by here. We were on our way to spend the evening with our son and his family and might not have gotten back until late."

She unlocked the front door and, reaching inside, flicked on the light.

"Come on in," she said, "and get warm."

In a minute or two her husband joined them. He entered the room unbuttoning his overcoat and slipping out of it. "I hope you didn't have to wait too long."

Alex shook his head.

"Oh, no. We had just driven up when you came along."

"Sit down, won't you? I'll only be a minute."

Joe and Nellie sat down on one side of the large room and Robin and Alex on the other. Robin looked around. The house had a comfortable, homey, well-worn look – the sort of place her grandparents lived in. It was a nice, friendly house. She was glad of that.

The justice of the peace came back into the room and sat down across from them. "So you want to get married, eh?"

"That's right," Alex said.

"You look a bit young. How old are you, young lady?"

He directed his question to Robin, but Alex was the one who quickly answered.

"It's all right. Here." He pulled the marriage license from his pocket and handed it to the justice of the peace. The man took the paper and read it over.

"Everything seems to be in order," he said, "but I must say that both of you look a lot younger than it says on this license."

Alex swallowed against the knot in his throat.

"We're both old enough to get married," he blustered.

Robin's face colored as he lied brazenly.

The justice of the peace folded the marriage license and tapped on his knee with it.

"What about your parents?" he asked. "Do they know about this?"

"Sure," Alex said. "We talked it over with them."

"And they gave you their permission?" He spoke doubtfully.

"They think it's a great idea. They didn't feel they could go to the expense of a big church wedding. Robin and I didn't want that either, so they told us to go ahead and get married this way."

"Hmmm." The man's expression became even more serious. "Tell me, have you seriously thought this thing through? Getting married is an important step in your lives. In fact, it's probably one of the most important things you'll ever do. Are you absolutely sure this is what you want?"

"Absolutely," Alex replied.

The justice of the peace turned to Robin. "And what about you, young lady?" he asked gently. "How do you feel about this? Are you certain you want to marry this young man?"

Robin's eyes grew starry. "Oh, yes."

"Do you love him?"

"More than anything or anyone else in the whole world." She looked over at Alex and smiled lovingly.

The justice tugged at the lobe of his ear. Then he turned to Nellie and Joe who were sitting in silence on the other side of the room.

"Are these young people your witnesses?"

"Yes, sir," Alex said. "This is Mr. and Mrs. Chamberlain. They were married just a couple of months ago."

"You two look pretty young to be married too," the justice of the peace said. "Guess they're getting married a lot younger these days."

The justice of the peace turned toward the door to his den. "I'll get the book with the ceremony in it and be right back."

Alex reached over and squeezed Robin's hand. "Just think," he said, "in a few minutes we'll be married. Won't that be wonderful?"

Nellie giggled softly.

"You should have seen us on our wedding day. We forgot to have any attendants along and had to get some little old couple from up the street."

Nellie continued to give all the details of their own elopement, but Robin wasn't really listening. She was thinking about the note she had left for her parents, telling them she loved Alex with all her heart and had decided to marry him that very night.

Subconsciously she toyed with the lovely corsage of red roses Alex had given her.

Just then the tall justice came back into the room.

"Well," he said, "I think we're ready."

* * *

Back in Fairview Mr. and Mrs. Smith had come over to the Evans home and the four of them were trying to decide what to do next.

"There's probably nothing to worry about," Alex's dad said. "The kids may have gone out to an all-night cafe and got to talking and forgot what time it is. You know how kids are."

Richard Evans broke in. "I don't see how they could stay as late as this. Robin knows we'd be frantic."

"Or they might be parked on some lonely road."

Mrs. Evans protested quickly. "Not Robin." There was confidence in her voice. "She wouldn't park on a lonely road with any boy. She's not that kind of a girl."

Mrs. Smith spoke up. "And Alex isn't that kind of a boy either."

Mr. Evans opened the closet door and got out his hat and coat. "We aren't going to accomplish anything by standing here looking at one another. I'm going to drive around and see if I can find them."

"But what if they should come home and we're gone?"

Ed Smith put on his hat and turned to his wife.

"You and Mrs. Evans stay here. Richard and I will go out to look for them."

"You–you won't be gone long, will you?" his wife asked.

"We'll either come back or phone you in half an hour."

The two men went out to the Evans' car and got in. Richard backed out to the street.

"I suppose this is a waste of time," he said, "but it's better than sitting at home waiting for the phone to ring."

Mr. Smith nodded. "I sure hope we find those kids before long. Agnes is going to be in hysterics in a little while."

"It's shaking Gladys up too."

"I wouldn't be quite so concerned if it weren't for Agnes's heart," Alex's dad went on. "She had a heart attack last summer and has only been able to do her own work for the last month or so. This is mighty rough on her."

They drove past one of the all-night cafes, their eyes searching the parking lot which was practically empty.

"There's no sign of them here." Disappointment tinged Mr. Evans' voice.

"I hardly thought there would be. A couple of kids couldn't find enough in a cafe to keep them occupied until this hour."

Richard turned at the next corner and circled back to the other side of town. "I keep trying to tell myself that they're all right, but I can't help worrying about them. Robin has never stayed out as late as this in her whole life."

"Alex is usually home earlier than this too. It sort of makes you wonder if they did have an accident or were parked on some lovers' lane and some guy hit them over the head or something."

Mr. Evans was about to pull out onto the highway when he stopped a second time suddenly.

"Ed," he said, "do you see someone over there?"

His passenger stared in the direction he was pointing. "Who is it?" he demanded. "Alex and Robin?"

"No, it's not them, but I thought it looked like that Gilbert boy Danny and Kay Orlis are taking care of."

Mr. Smith spoke slowly. "It did look like a kid, at that."

"I thought for sure it was him, but I must've been mistaken. Danny wouldn't let him run around at this hour."

"Not if he's any kind of a guardian at all."

They drove by the other all-night restaurants but found no trace of Alex and Robin. Finally they stopped and called home. Mrs. Evans answered breathlessly.

"Oh, it's you, Richard!" Disappointment was heavy in her voice.

"Yes, it's me. I don't suppose you've heard anything from the kids yet?"

"No, when the phone rang just now, I was sure it must be Robin."

"We've got a couple of more places to check. Then we'll be home as soon as we can."

Mr. Smith tapped him on the shoulder. "Find out how Agnes is doing."

Mrs. Evans heard him. "She's been crying ever since you left. I finally got her to lie down." Her voice broke.

"Gladys!" Richard Evans exclaimed, "are you all right?"

At first she did not reply.

"Gladys!" he repeated. "What's wrong?"

She did not sound like herself when she answered.

"Richard! What has happened to Robin?"

CHAPTER 7

ROBIN AND ALEX COME HOME

Neither Mr. and Mrs. Evans nor Mr. and Mrs. Smith were able to sleep at all that night. They sat in the kitchen of the Evans home, sipping coffee and looking miserably at one another. They had long since run out of anything to say.

Every now and then Ed Smith studied his wife's ashen face. "Feel all right, dear?" he asked, trying to mask the concern in his voice.

"Don't worry about me."

Once again silence gripped them.

At long last Richard Evans voiced the question that lay unspoken on each heart.

"What do we do now?"

Mr. Smith's lips parted slightly, and he tugged nervously at the lobe of his ear. But he did not speak.

"Would it do any good to call the police again?" Robin's mother asked. "Or the hospital? Isn't there a chance by this time that they might have heard something?"

Her husband shook his head. "I don't think so. If they had, they'd have notified us right away. We've called both places twice and left our names and phone number."

Mrs. Evans' voice rose hysterically. "I don't see how we can sit here talking about Robin and Alex so calmly. Richard! We've got to do something."

He stared at her. "What more can we do?" he asked.

Mr. Smith glanced at the tension in his wife's face.

"I don't think the kids have had an accident," he said. "It's more likely that they've had some car trouble and haven't been able to call."

Mr. Evans paced across the kitchen floor. "I'd like to believe that," he said, "but it's hardly likely. Robin's car is practically new." The lines in his face deepened. "No, there's got to be another reason."

Mrs. Smith grasped her husband by the arm.

"What do you think has happened?"

Slowly he shook his head.

"I wish I knew," he answered. "I only wish I knew."

"What are the police being paid for?" she asked. "Can't they help us?"

"About all they could do is to issue a pickup order. And before they'll do that, we'd have to sign a complaint so they could make out a warrant."

"Against our own son?" Mrs. Smith asked incredulously.

"They'd have to have some legal reason for arresting them."

Mrs. Smith started to cry again quietly. Tears came to Gladys Evans' eyes. Bravely she fought against them.

Mr. Evans noted the time.

"Let's wait a couple of more hours," he said, "before we do anything more. If the kids have had car trouble, that will give them plenty of time to get a hold of us."

They lapsed into silence. It was some minutes later when Mrs. Smith spoke up suddenly. "You don't suppose they've gone off and gotten married, do you?"

The others jerked upright.

"What?" Mr. Evans demanded.

"They could have," she went on. "They've certainly been crazy about each other. I've never seen Alex so taken with a girl as he has been with Robin."

Mrs. Evans protested quickly. "But Robin would never do a thing like that," she said. "Why–why, she isn't old enough to get married. She's just a child!"

"Alex hasn't even finished high school," Mr. Smith said. "To tell you the truth, I've been corresponding with my old alma mater about him. I haven't said anything to him about it yet. I was afraid it would make him conceited, but they're so anxious to have him come and play football for them they'll give him a scholarship. If he got married now, it would ruin everything."

Mrs. Smith got to her feet. "Did you look for a note in Robin's room?" she insisted.

Mr. Evans was the first one to reach Robin's bedroom. The others were close behind him.

"There's no note on the bed," he said.

"What about her suitcase and clothes?" Mrs. Smith continued. "Are they here?"

Richard Evans jerked open the closet door.

"Where does she keep her suitcase, Gladys?"

"On the top shelf."

There was a taut silence.

"It's gone!"

Mrs. Evans' face went ashen. "And so is her new taffeta dress!"

Mrs. Smith grasped her husband's arm and swayed slightly. He guided her over to a chair and helped her into it.

Mr. Evans went to the dresser and began to look around. "Robin wouldn't run away and not leave a note," he said. "I know her well enough for that." He was about to turn away when he caught a glimpse of the corner of an envelope under the mirror.

"What's that?" Ed demanded.

The girl's father opened the envelope and read aloud: "Dear Mom and Dad, Alex and I love each other so much that we can't live apart any longer. By the time you read this, we will be married. Please try to understand—"

There was more, but both Mrs. Smith and Mrs. Evans burst into tears.

* * *

Before noon both sets of parents had messages from the newly married couple, and Sunday afternoon they came home. They went to Robin's house first.

Mrs. Evans threw her arms around her daughter's neck and cried a little. So did Robin.

"Don't cry, Mom. Please."

"I–I can't help it."

"But Alex and I are so happy," she protested. "And we want you to be happy too."

The Smiths came over as soon as possible after Mr. Evans called them. There was a brief reunion and then Alex and Robin faced their parents. Mr. Evans turned to his daughter accusingly.

"Robin," he said, "why did you do it?"

A tear trickled down her cheek.

"We love each other, Daddy," she told him.

"We could have this marriage annulled, you know."

Fear sprang to her eyes. "You wouldn't!"

"You're underage, and you didn't have our permission to be married. That's grounds enough for an annulment."

"If you don't want us around, Daddy," she said, "we–we can go away somewhere."

His face softened.

"That wouldn't solve anything."

"Neither would an annulment. We love each other! Don't you understand?"

His gaze met hers. There was a long silence.

"Robin," he said finally, "we don't want to throw you and Alex out. We want what's best for both of you."

Alex spoke up quickly. "Well, you won't be helping us by trying to get the marriage annulled," he said. "I can tell you that much right now."

Up until that moment Mr. Evans had not spoken to his daughter's young husband. Now he faced him.

"Tell me something, Alex," he said, "can you support Robin?"

A peculiar look came over the boy's face as though he had never before thought about that.

"Do you think you can pay rent, food, clothing, and all the other living costs that are the responsibility of the head of a household?" Richard went on.

"I–I guess so," the boy said lamely.

"Just how do you plan to do it?"

Alex ran his hand nervously across his handsome young face. "Get a job, I guess."

"What about school?"

There was a brief silence.

"I–I thought maybe I could get a part-time job until after school is out. Then I could–" His voice trailed away.

"It's not going to be easy for you, Alex," his dad said. "But I hope you'll plan to stay in school."

"Sure, Dad," he said confidently. "I'll finish school. We've never planned anything else."

"But what about Robin's car payments and her other obligations that we have been paying?" Mr. Evans asked. "Those are your responsibility now."

Robin spoke up meekly. "Daddy, it'll only be a few months until school is out. Then Alex and I can both go to work. Could–couldn't you help us until then?"

Her dad was serious. "We'll do all we can, but there's a limit to what we can do." He breathed deeply. "I suppose the first thing is to find a small, inexpensive apartment."

The young bride brightened. "They have some darling apartments over on Park Lane."

Her dad protested quickly. "Those 'darling apartments,' as you call them, rent for one thousand dollars a month. We'll have to find something cheaper than that."

Mr. Smith nodded. "It will take some looking, but I think we can find an inexpensive unfurnished apartment. We have some furniture in the basement that will serve for a while."

Alex snorted indignantly. "That junk?"

"You'll probably be very happy to have 'that junk' before you can afford to buy furniture of your own."

Robin looked from one to the other helplessly. This was so different from what she had thought the start of their married life would be!

Mrs. Evans turned to her husband. "I suppose the children could move in with us temporarily. At least until Alex gets through school."

"Or with us," Mrs. Smith added quickly.

Richard Evans shook his head. "I don't think it's wise. There are enough adjustments for a newly married couple to make without living in the same house with either set of parents."

Mr. Smith nodded his head. "I agree with that," he said. "If they can manage in any other way."

Mr. Evans thought for a moment. "I have a friend in the real estate business. He may have some cheap apartments listed. If Alex and Robin can find something reasonable, we can probably help them, at least for a while."

He called the real estate broker and got the addresses of a number of furnished and unfurnished apartments. They went to the nearest one, a small dark apartment on the second floor. Robin looked about distastefully.

"It's so dingy and small," she said, shuddering. "And the living room window looks out on the alley. Can't we find something better than this?"

The landlord glanced in her direction, his lips curling.

"Not at no four hundred dollars a month, you won't. The fact is, I doubt if you'll be able to find another four hundred dollar apartment in town."

The second place was six hundred dollars a month. It was a little bigger than the first apartment and had a private bath, but it still was nothing like either the Evans or the Smith home.

Robin turned plaintively to her mother. "I had no idea that apartment rent would be so high."

"Everything's expensive these days, dear."

"Alex and I had our hearts set on one of the Park Lane apartments," she went on plaintively. "They look so cute."

After checking all the apartments the real estate agent had listed, they settled on one not far from school that rented for five hundred and fifty dollars a month. Mr. Evans and Mr. Smith both agreed that it was the best one available for the money.

"It's close to school and downtown," Richard said. "And that's important."

Robin spoke up quickly. "It wouldn't matter too much where we live. We'll have the car to get around in."

An odd look came to her dad's eyes.

"Won't we?"

"We'll talk about the car later, Robin."

"I don't see what our getting married has to do with the car. You gave it to me. It's mine."

Mr. Evans was a long while in answering.

"I gave you the car, Robin. That's true. But when I did, I didn't know this was going to happen. We're going to try to keep it for you, but we may have to sell it in order to have money enough to help you and Alex get through school."

CHAPTER 8

THE SCHOOL CAUSES TROUBLE

That night Robin and Alex sat for a long while in the living room at the Evans' home, talking quietly. Her parents had long since gone to bed.

"I wouldn't get so upset about the car if I were you, Robin," Alex said. "I'm sure your dad's going to feel differently about it after he's had time to think it over."

Her small fingers worked nervously at the hem of her shirt.

"Oh, Alex," she said, "I thought everything was going to be so wonderful when we came back. I could just see us having one of those cute apartments with beautiful new furniture and–and everything. Instead, we're going to be living in that ugly old Jacobs' house."

"It's not so bad."

"Not so bad?" she echoed. "It–it's horrible."

"We won't have to live there very long. As soon

as I get out of school, I'll get a good job. Then we'll be able to move into one of those new apartments or maybe even into our own home."

"I–I'm sorry, Alex. I didn't mean to complain. I really don't care what kind of an apartment we have to live in or even if we've got the car. Just so we have each other."

"That's the way I feel too. Everything will work out all right. You wait and see."

The next morning they went to school a bit earlier than usual. As soon as they appeared in the corridor, the kids began to cluster around and ply them with questions.

"Is it true that you two got married?" one of the guys asked.

The young couple beamed.

"That's right."

Disappointment smoked the boy's eyes. "Man, is the coach ever mad at you!"

"Why?"

"He said that you won't get to play basketball anymore."

Alex caught his breath sharply.

"Why not? I figure on staying in school, and I'll be keeping my grades up – maybe better than I did before."

"I don't know, but that's not the way I got it from him. He said you wouldn't be able to play."

"I'll go in and talk to him," Alex blustered. "I'll have to get that straightened out."

Robin's hand tightened on his big fingers.

"Do–do you want me to go along?" she asked, her voice trembling.

"No, go on into the principal's office and get your pass back to classes. I'll be there in a few minutes."

The coach was sitting alone in his office when Alex entered.

"Hello, Coach."

His gaze met Alex's icily. "I see you're back."

"Thought I'd stop by and tell you that I'll be out for practice tonight," he said carelessly.

The coach's expression did not change. "Have you cleared that with the principal?"

For the first time fear flickered in Alex's eyes. "What do you mean?"

"Just what I said. Have you cleared that with the principal's office?"

"I–I was going in there after I–I'd talked with you."

"You came to the wrong place first." With that the coach turned his attention deliberately to the papers on his desk.

Alex stood there trying to think of something to say, but he could not. After a moment he turned and went to the principal's office. Robin was still sitting in the waiting room. She got up as he came in.

"Mr. Brown said I should wait for you, Alex. He wants to talk to us together."

Before the boy could reply, the office door opened, and the principal motioned to them.

"I'll see you now." He ushered them into his office

and closed the door behind them. "I understand you two were married."

"Th-th-that's right," Alex stammered.

"I suppose you want to see about coming back to school."

"Y-yes, sir."

The principal picked up a pencil and held it. "I know how you feel about coming back to school. And I know how important it is to have you finish your education. Believe me. But–"

Robin broke in quickly.

"You're going to let us come back, aren't you?"

"You're on the basketball team, aren't you, Alex?" he asked.

"That's right."

"Are there any other extracurricular activities you're in?"

"I'm president of the senior class and was planning on trying out for the class play. Then, of course, I'll be out for track in the spring."

"If you stay in school, Alex, you will not be allowed to play basketball, continue as class president, or take part in any other outside activities."

"What?"

"That is the policy of the school board in marriages between students. It is the only way you can continue to work toward your diploma."

The color drained from Alex' face. "I–I–" But he could find no words to speak.

* * *

When Danny Orlis came home that night, Jim Morgan was waiting for him excitedly.

"Did you hear the news, Danny?" he asked.

"What kind of news?"

"About Alex Smith and Robin Evans. They ran away the other night and got married."

Danny took off his coat and hung it in the closet.

"I'm sorry to hear that," he said.

"And that's not all. Alex isn't going to get to play any more basketball. He had to quit the team and turn in his uniform and everything."

"I'm not surprised. I think most school boards have laid down regulations like that. They won't let boys who are married take part in any outside activities."

"Man, he was our best player. Everybody in school is mad at him now!"

Kay came to the door just then and called them to dinner. They went into the kitchen and started to sit down when she noticed Kent's hands.

"Kent," she said quietly, "don't you think you'd better go and wash? Your hands are awfully dirty."

He sat down at the table defiantly. "I did wash 'em."

Danny turned to him, his face stern. "Kent, you heard what Kay said."

"But I did wash my hands just a minute ago. They ain't so bad. See?" He thrust them out.

"Go and wash them again and don't come back to the table until they're clean. Understand?"

Kent pushed his chair back noisily and got to his feet.

"Okay. Okay. But I wish you'd quit pickin' on me. That's what I wish." He was still grumbling to himself as he disappeared into the bathroom and closed the door.

They had almost finished eating when Kay spoke up.

"I went over to see Mrs. Evans this afternoon, Danny," she said. "She's terribly broken up by Robin's marriage."

"I can imagine she is."

"She says it isn't that she and Richard object to Alex as a person. He's a good, clean-cut boy. But she's certain that Alex has never put his trust in Christ for salvation."

"Yes, and getting married while they're still in school is going to be hard for all of them, but especially for Robin and Alex. It's tough enough to earn a living these days without trying to get an education at the same time."

There was a brief silence. Finally Jim spoke up. "You know, Danny, I can't figure this out."

"You can't figure what out?" Danny asked.

"Robin was the leading Christian in our youth group and probably the best Christian in our school. Now she runs off and marries a guy like Alex who isn't even a Christian. How can you explain that?"

Danny took his time in answering.

"I don't know for sure why it happened, Jim," he said, "but I've got a good idea. You remember that Robin felt called to the mission field and her parents were opposed to it?"

"Yeah?"

"She listened to them and turned her back on the Lord. When any Christian does that, he soon gets out of the Lord's will and that's when Satan gets a foothold. To me, what happened is a tragic example."

Jim tugged thoughtfully at the lobe of his ear.

"That does make sense. You know, I'll bet Mr. and Mrs. Evans wish now that they'd let her go to prepare for the mission field. They'd sure be a lot happier."

"I think everyone concerned would be a lot happier," Danny went on. "That's the way it usually is when we get outside the will of God."

* * *

The next few days at school Robin was something of a celebrity among the girls. They crowded around her at every opportunity, talking excitedly about her new home.

"Oh, I'm so happy for you," one junior girl said.

Robin smiled breathlessly. "I'm sort of happy for myself and for Alex," she said.

"I'm so anxious to see your new apartment. It must be darling."

"Yes," somebody else put in. "We all want to come up and see you."

Robin's face clouded. "Wait until we've had a chance to get the curtains up and some pictures hung and that sort of thing. Then we'll want you all to come up and see us."

"Don't worry, we'll be there. You won't have to give us a second invitation."

One of the other senior girls spoke up. "George and I were talking about you last night. I told him we ought to do like you and Alex did and get married right away, but no. He's so determined to go on to college and get his degree in engineering that he can't think of anything else."

Robin flushed. "Oh, Alex is planning to go on to school too. He may have to wait a semester. But after we've had a chance to save a little money, he's going on to college."

The girls went on down the corridor to their first class, still plying Robin with questions. Starry-eyed, she answered them. In the classroom she took her seat across from Linda Penner, who looked up at her and smiled.

"Hello, Robin."

"Hi."

"I want to wish you all the happiness in the world."

"Thank you."

"I'll be praying for you – and for Alex," she went on softly.

Robin straightened, and her smile faded. What was the matter with Linda, talking that way? She was probably jealous. That was all. Jealous because she hadn't been able to find anyone like Alex and get married.

"Are you coming to Bible club tonight?" Linda asked.

"I don't know." Robin's voice was cold and distant. "I'll have to ask Alex. We decide everything together, you know."

At that instant, Tom Channing came up.

"Hi, Linda." He glanced over at Robin. "Hello, Robin. Congratulations."

"Thanks."

Tom turned his attention to Linda. "Guess what? I got my acceptance from Cedarton Bible Institute yesterday, so I'll probably be going there next fall. The only thing lacking now are my grades for this semester. If they're okay, I'm in."

"That's great, Tom. I'm a little behind you, though. I just sent for a catalog last week."

They talked on excitedly about going to school the next year. Robin tried not to listen, but she couldn't help it. She had once planned on going to CBI the following year as well. She had even written to a friend in Minneapolis to see if they could room together, but now that was all over. Even if Alex did get to go to college, it wouldn't be to Cedarton. He always said he was going to some big-name school where they had a good, strong football team.

For an instant disappointment welled within her. Moments later she scolded herself for allowing such thoughts to come to mind. Even though she wouldn't be able to go to Bible school, she told herself, it was worth it. She loved Alex more than anything or anyone else in the whole world. Being married to him was wonderful. And at the moment she didn't even count the cost.

When she got home from school that afternoon, she thought Alex would be there waiting for her. But he wasn't. It was 6:30 when he finally came in, a scowl marring his handsome young face.

"Alex," she said accusingly. "You're late. I–I've had dinner ready for an hour."

He dropped dejectedly to the worn sofa.

"I've been out trying to find a job. I don't think there's any part-time work in this whole town! I've been everywhere."

"I saw a couple of ads this morning."

"Sure!" Disappointment and anger tinged his voice. "Sure. You saw a couple of ads this morning. So did I. And I checked them both out. They're for full-time work. But that's not all. Do you know what the requirements were? One of them wants a man with a college degree. The other wants someone with at least two years of college and three years of experience. Those are the kind of guys who can get jobs."

Robin sat down on the arm of the sofa and put her hand on his shoulder.

"This is the first day you've gone out looking for

something to do," she said encouragingly. "Don't get so disappointed so easily. You'll find something."

He looked up at her. "And what do we do until I do?" he asked. "Take handouts from our parents?"

The next evening after school Robin waited for Alex just outside the front door. When he came out, she saw that he looked troubled.

"What's the matter, Alex?" she asked.

"Nothing."

"I know better."

They crossed the street to the school parking lot. It was not until they were in the car and headed home that Alex spoke again.

"I went down to the gym a little while ago," he said. "I was just going to shoot a few baskets and watch the guys practice. I wouldn't have hurt a thing. But the coach kicked me out. He wouldn't even let me stay and watch the practice game."

"That's mean."

"They've got it in for me, that's all," he stormed. "For two cents I'd quit school, that's what I'd do."

"Oh, Alex, don't do that!" she exclaimed. "Don't even think about quitting school."

"I won't," he told her, grinning at her concern. "I just said that I felt like quitting school. Just because we got married is no reason they have to treat us as though we've got leprosy or something."

He pulled up before their apartment house and stopped.

"Alex," Robin said, "I was talking with Linda Penner. She invited us to Bible club at Danny and Kay's tonight."

He shook his head. "Nothing doing! I'm not going there and have all the kids staring at me as though I'm some kind of freak."

"They won't do that. They're our friends."

"Just the same, I'm not going!"

CHAPTER 9

ALEX GOES TO CHURCH

The Fairview basketball team, after a whirlwind start, lost the next five games in a row, the last by a whopping margin. Almost everybody in school blamed Alex for the defeats.

"If you were just playing, Alex," one of the underclassmen said to him, "we'd still be undefeated."

"Oh, I don't know."

"Yes, we would. There isn't another guy on the whole squad who can shoot the way you can. If you just hadn't gotten married until after the basketball season was over, we'd have won the conference."

"It's not my fault they won't let me play," he said defensively. "Of all the stupid rules, the one about not letting a married guy take part in outside activities is the worst! What difference does it make? That's what I'd like to know."

"Search me."

At home that evening he again talked with Robin about it.

"It isn't fair. There isn't anything fair about it." He got up and paced across the threadbare rug. "I think they've got it in for me. That's what I think."

Robin agreed. "Just because we had the courage to go ahead and get married is no reason they ought to pick on us," she said.

"I think I'll go to the school board about it," Alex told her. "I'm not going to let them keep shoving me around. I've got some rights too."

There was a short silence.

"Maybe if we talked with Dad, he could get something done about it."

Alex whirled, eyes blazing. "Maybe Daddy could do something!" He exploded hotly. "All I hear any more is maybe Daddy can fix it!' He's not the only one in the world who can do things!"

Robin caught her breath and tears trembled on her eyelids.

"A-A-Alex, that's the first time you've ever been angry with me or have even spoken a cross word at me."

Slowly his anger seeped away, and he came over to her.

"I'm sorry, Robin. I didn't mean to explode, but I get so mad when I think of the way they've been treating us at school that I can't think straight."

Robin's voice was thin and quavering. "I–I know."

He dried her tears.

"But we don't care," he continued. "If I don't get to play basketball, I don't get to play basketball. That's all. We have each other. That's all that really matters."

Robin pulled away from him momentarily to look into his eyes.

"Is that honestly the way you feel, Alex?" she asked, her voice tremoring. "You're not just saying that?"

"It's honestly the way I feel. I don't care if I never get to shoot another basket. I have you. That's all I really care about."

"Oh, Alex." She melted into his arms, and for a moment clung there crying.

"Hey, now. That's enough of that. Dry those tears and show me a smile for a change."

"I–I just can't help it."

The following Sunday morning Alex reluctantly agreed to go to Sunday school and church with his bride.

"But I wish you'd go to *my* church, Robin," he said.

She came into the living room. "Why?"

"I feel more comfortable there for one thing. That preacher of yours makes a guy feel like seventeen different kinds of sinner. I don't like it."

She smiled inwardly. Alex was under conviction. That was why he felt the way he did about going to her church with her. The Holy Spirit must be dealing with him. Her heart sang.

"That's because he preaches the Bible," she answered.

"They preach the Bible over at our church too, but they use some common sense about it."

They went to church a few minutes before time for Sunday school and entered the foyer. The Sunday school usher greeted them warmly. "And what class do you want to attend?"

Robin stared blankly at him. "I–I don't know," she said. "We hadn't thought much about that."

The usher hesitated. "You could go into the young married couples' class, but–but–"

Robin spoke up quickly. "We do not want to go in there. Most of them are eight or ten years older than we are."

"You could go in with the college kids – or the high school seniors."

Robin turned to Alex.

"Where do you think we ought to go?"

"How should I know?" he snapped. "This is your church."

"Maybe we could go into my old class – if that's all right."

"I don't care." By this time Alex' face was flushed. "Just so we get out of here where everybody's watching us."

As they went down the basement stairs, he turned to her and mumbled.

"If I'd known anything like this had been going to happen, I wouldn't have come."

They sat in the back of the room during the class.

As soon as the lesson ended, Alex guided her out on the sidewalk in front of the church.

"I don't know about you, Robin, but I'm going home."

"But, Alex," she protested. "We were going to stay for church."

"Maybe you are, but I'm not! I'm getting out of here!"

"But you promised!"

"That was before I knew what that Sunday school class was going to be like. I'm not going to stick around here any longer and be insulted."

"Nobody insulted you." She spoke defensively. "Mr. Franzen wasn't even talking about you."

Alex's voice raised. "No, he wasn't talking *about* me. He was talking to me! He kept talking about being a sinner and headed for hell unless we confess our sin and put our trust in Jesus. I could feel everybody in the class looking at me. I'm not coming back, Robin. I can tell you that much right now. You'll never get me inside this church again!"

Robin spoke in a tense whisper.

"Alex," she said, "don't talk so loud. People will hear you."

"It didn't make any difference to that bald-headed Franzen when he talked to me in front of everybody," Alex stormed. "I don't care who hears me either. I had a notion to get up and walk right out of there while he was talking."

Anger flamed in Robin's eyes.

"Somebody's coming, Alex. Please!"

As the gray-haired couple approached, Alex stopped talking and, as they neared, he spoke to them as graciously as though he and Robin had not been quarreling.

Robin smiled her gratitude and squeezed his hand.

"You will go into church with me, won't you, Alex?"

Momentarily he hesitated.

"I suppose so. But I can tell you this much. Don't ask me to go again. I've had it!"

They turned and walked slowly back into the building and found a seat near the door.

In another part of the sanctuary Kent Gilbert scooted down in the seat beside Danny Orlis, a scowl twisting his young face.

"Kent," Danny whispered, "sit up."

"What're you kickin' about?" the boy demanded. "I'm here, ain't I?"

For answer Danny grasped him firmly by the shoulder and pulled him upright.

"For cryin' out loud!" he exclaimed. "Can't I even sit without you naggin' at me?"

CHAPTER 10

ROBIN BECOMES A HOMEMAKER

Alex tried hard to get a part-time job in Fairview. As soon as school was out, he went directly uptown and continued to make the rounds. But it was useless. Nobody needed extra help. That evening when he came home, he was despondent. Robin met him at the door.

"Hi, Alex," she said brightly.

"Hi." Dejection was in every move.

He came in slowly and took off his jacket, dropping it on the couch.

"How did it go?" she asked.

He shook his head. "Not worth a cent. I tell you, Robin, there just isn't any use in trying anymore. There isn't any part-time work around this stupid town."

Dejectedly Alex leaned forward and buried his head in his hands. Robin came over and sat on the couch beside him.

"Were you at Millers'?" she asked.

"I was at Millers'," he repeated, "the Economy Department Store, all the garages, service stations, farm implement places, and the supermarkets. I tell you, I've been every place that I could even think of. I've practically pleaded for work – any kind of work." His voice trailed away. And for a time all was silent. "But I couldn't find a thing. Not a single, solitary thing."

She put her arm around his shoulder sympathetically and tried not to show her own concern.

"I know you've tried hard, Alex, but don't let it get you so discouraged. If we just keep looking around, something will turn up. You wait and see."

His gaze met hers. "That's what I've been telling myself every time I've come back from looking for work. Don't get upset. There's a job somewhere in Fairview. Just don't get discouraged. But I haven't been able to come up with anything. Not even a job sweeping out a store after they've closed for the day. I can't find anything to do."

"I know." She swallowed hard. "I know. But there *has* to be some work somewhere. There just has to be."

He ran his fingers through his hair.

"I promised our dads that I'd get work and take over as much of the load as possible, but I haven't earned more than a few dollars since we got married."

"It's getting closer to spring, Alex," she said. "I'm sure that you'll be able to find something to do when it warms up, if you haven't found work before."

"Maybe." But doubt edged his voice. "I'm beginning to think that there's something wrong with me that makes people not want to hire me."

"Alex!"

"It's true, Robin. I've been practically every place in town and haven't been able to find anything yet. Not even anything that sounds as though it might develop into a job. I tell you, Robin, I've never been so discouraged in my life."

There was a long, painful silence.

"Alex." Her voice was small and weak.

"Yes?"

"Alex, I hate to ask you this."

"What is it now?" Irritation curled his lips.

"Did you see your dad today?"

"No, why?" By this time he was sitting up straight and staring directly into her eyes. "What's this all about, Robin?"

"The man who owns the apartment was up to see you," she said hesitantly. "The rent was due three days ago."

Alex sighed deeply. "I should've known. This is rough on our parents, you know. They had a rough time financially before we got married. It's really going to strip them to have to keep paying out money for our rent and food and–and even our spending money."

He got to his feet.

"I think that gets me more than anything else. Even having to go to them for spending money! Here I am, a married man, and if my wife wants to put five gallons of gas in the car her dad gave her, or if we want a candy bar, we've got to ask our parents to pay for it."

The muscles in Robin's throat tightened, but she managed a crooked little smile. "Now, Alex," she answered. "It's not as bad as it sounds when you put it that way. Things are hard for us now, but it's only until we graduate from school and you can get a good job. Then everything will be all right."

Deliberately he turned back to her.

"If I got a chance to get a full-time job right now, I believe I'd take it."

Her eyes widened. "Oh, Alex!" she exclaimed. "No!"

He came back and sat down.

"I don't have any chance of a job," he said miserably. "Any kind of a job, so there's nothing for you to worry about. I don't think there's anyone in town who'll hire me for anything."

Robin tried desperately to cheer him up, but it was no use. She had never seen anyone so despondent before.

* * *

Robin found the first few weeks of her marriage to Alex most exciting. She was never alone at school. The moment she came into the classroom the girls clustered around her, talking to her about their apartment or asking her questions.

100

Just when the change came, she didn't know. It was so subtle she scarcely realized it until she suddenly became aware of the fact that the girls were no longer interested in her or the things she and Alex did. They spoke to her the same as they always had, but it wasn't the same. And it seemed that they had but very little to talk with her about. At home that evening she decided to talk it over with Alex.

"I can't understand it," she said. "Do you suppose I've said something or done something to make them mad at me?"

He pulled her down on the couch beside him.

"If you want my opinion," he said jokingly, "they're all jealous of you because you got me."

But she was in no mood for joking. She sat up straight. "I did promise to have them over as soon as we got the apartment fixed up," she said, "and I haven't done it. Maybe that's what's wrong."

She eyed him carefully. "Do you suppose it would be all right for me to have some of the girls in one night this week?"

"I don't know." The furrows in his forehead deepened. "It costs money to have company."

"I could get a cake mix from Mom and make some jello or something simple like that," she said.

"And what am I supposed to be doing while all this is going on?" he asked her irritably.

"You could be here. I don't plan on having more than just a few. I think you'd enjoy it."

He snorted his indignation. "Me stay here while you're having a party with those stupid, giggling friends of yours? I'd go nuts."

Her temper flared. "They're no worse than your friends."

There was a short silence.

"If you didn't want to stay here, Alex, you could go over to see your parents and watch TV."

"Who wants to do that?"

"I don't know why you're so unreasonable. You get to go out and see some of your old friends after school."

Alex retorted hotly. "That's what you think."

"Well, you do," she said angrily. "I have to come home and–and clean and wash clothes and–and cook. You can go down to the snack shop and loaf around with your friends."

"Ha! I don't know how I could go down and loaf. I've been out every blasted night after school trying to find a job. Besides, I don't even have money for a bottle of pop. I couldn't hang around the snack shop very long. I'll clue you in on that."

Her eyes flamed. "Well, it's not my fault!"

"Who said it was?"

"You certainly act like it. Every time I say anything to you lately you throw it up to me that you haven't even got any money for candy or ice cream. You act as though I'm the one who's responsible."

He stood upright. By this time his face was white and drawn.

"Maybe it's not your fault, but I can tell you this much. Things weren't this way before I married you. That's for sure!"

She stared miserably at him. Tears trembled on her eyelids.

"Oh, Alex! I–I never thought I'd hear you talk to me this way."

She buried her head in her hands and began to sob quietly. For two or three minutes she did not move. Neither did Alex. At last he edged closer to her.

"I–I shouldn't have said that, Robin," he told her clumsily. "I didn't really mean it. I was just mad and was trying to hurt you."

"I know you didn't mean it," she told him, dabbing at her eyes. "But this–" She swallowed forcibly. "This is the first time we've ever quarreled and I–I didn't think I could stand it."

He sat down beside her and took her in his arms.

"Let's not quarrel again, Robin. Ever."

She nodded, a faint smile lifting the corners of her mouth. "I don't want to ever quarrel with you, Alex. I don't care if I *ever* get to have any of the girls over to the apartment."

"You've got to have friends," he told her. "It was selfish of me to say anything about it. You can have company in anytime you want to."

Her young face lit up. "Do you really mean it?"

"Of course I mean it."

"You're so sweet." Impulsively she kissed him.

* * *

The next day Robin went right home after school.

She had planned on talking with some of the girls about coming over one night the next week, but there was a senior class meeting, and she couldn't take time to go to it or to wait until it was over. It seemed as though she never got her work done anymore. At the moment there was laundry that should have been done a week ago. The floor was a mess and the sink in the kitchen was stacked with dirty dishes. She would have to do them before they could even have supper.

It wasn't that she didn't want to keep her house clean. There were times when she felt like screaming just to look at it. But she had her studies to do, and Alex wanted to go over to his parents to watch television almost every night. That sort of thing put her so far behind, that when they overslept, as they had that morning, she was swamped with work.

At the back stairs entrance to their apartment, she paused and wearily brushed her hair back from her eyes. When school had started last September, she wouldn't have been caught dead going to class without styling her hair every day. She still felt just as badly about it, but more and more often there absolutely wasn't time to do her hair. And if she did have the time, she was so weary she couldn't bring herself to do it. Instead, with increasing frequency, she began to push a comb through it and hope for the best.

Robin stepped into the little apartment and looked around. Alex had been there. His letter sweater was thrown carelessly across the faded couch, and one of his shoes was in the middle of the floor. The other he had kicked across the room and it had come to rest beside the baseboard.

Tears came into her eyes as she hung her own coat in the closet and began to pick up after him. Why couldn't he take the time to put his own clothes away? Why did he have to leave everything for her to do?

Briefly her temper flared.

All he did was go to school. He didn't even have a job. Why should she have to keep up her studies and do all of the cleaning and washing and cooking alone?

It wasn't fair. It just wasn't fair at all. He wouldn't even help her with the dishes. Marriage wasn't supposed to be one-sided. Both partners were supposed to contribute to it. It wasn't that she didn't love Alex. She did. But that was no sign she was supposed to be a slave.

She curled up on the couch and began to sniffle. Time ceased to exist for her. She was still sitting there when she heard footsteps on the stairs. It was Alex and he was coming home for dinner.

She couldn't let him see her in tears!

Robin leaped to her feet and, running hurriedly into the bathroom, began to wash her face.

He stopped just inside the door and called out to her, "Hi! You home?"

"I'm in here," she called. "I'll be out in a minute!"

He sauntered across the floor to the couch and dropped to it.

"This hole's getting filthy, Robin." he exclaimed, picking up his shirt. "You've sure been letting things go lately."

Anger surged through her, and it was only with difficulty that she was able to control herself.

"Have you forgotten? I have studying to do besides doing all the housework."

If Alex saw the storm signals, he ignored them.

"My mother never lets things get into a mess like this," he said, wrinkling his nose distastefully. "I sure hope she doesn't come over and see it before you get it cleaned up. She'll think you're a terrible housekeeper."

Robin's eyes flashed.

"Your mother didn't have to go to school, cook, clean house, pick up–"

"Maybe not," he continued, "but she had three kids to take care of."

That did it!

"You!" Robin exploded. "Oh, you!" She whirled and dashed into the bedroom and slammed the door.

Her young husband stared after her.

For several minutes Alex waited for her to stop crying and come back out to the living room, but she did not. At last, uneasily, he went over to the bedroom door and called out softly, "Robin."

There was no answer. All he could hear were the strident tones of music playing.

He shifted uneasily from one foot to the other and raised his voice. "Robin, I didn't mean it. I–I'm terribly sorry."

Still she did not answer him. He waited another minute or two before pushing the door open and going in. Robin was lying across the bed, her thin shoulders twitching convulsively.

Alex sat down on the edge of the bed and clumsily put his hand on her shoulder.

"Robin, don't cry."

"Who's crying?"

"You are."

There was another silence. "You couldn't hear me. The music was playing."

"I know, but you were crying just the same." He fumbled for words. "I–I didn't mean it, Robin. I'm sorry."

She sat up and turned to face him, unmindful of her tear-stained cheeks.

"I–I didn't think you'd ever talk to me that way, Alex."

He apologized again.

"I'm terribly sorry, honestly I am." He swallowed hard. "I really didn't mean it, Robin. I spoke without thinking."

With that he took her in his arms. For some minutes they clung to each other without speaking. Then she pulled away.

"I–I have to do the dishes," she said. "If I don't, we can't have anything to eat tonight."

Alex stood up and took hold of her hand. "Come on," he said. "I'll help you."

She looked at him briefly, her lower lip quivering.

"You don't have to, you know."

"I know that. But it happens that I want to."

"Do you really mean it?"

"I really mean it."

They went out in the kitchen together and got to work.

Nevertheless, the pain in Robin's young heart continued to grow. They had never once quarreled seriously during the time they had dated. Oh, they'd had their little arguments, but they only lasted a moment or two. Somehow she had always thought that they were different than most people. They would never have an argument serious enough to be called a quarrel. In fact, she felt that their love was too great for them to even have an argument. And Alex, she had reasoned, was too kind ever to say an ungracious thing to her.

But now they had quarreled twice. And in such a short time. Of course, Alex had apologized, but the spell was broken. Things weren't the same anymore. She swallowed the lump that had come up in her throat. Would they ever be the same again?

Once they finished the dishes, she shooed him out of the kitchen while she got supper. She wished that she had gotten something besides hamburger for them tonight, but that was the easiest to fix and she had been feeling sorry for herself.

When they were ready, she called Alex to the table. He came into the kitchen and looked around, wrinkling his nose distastefully.

"Hamburgers?" he echoed. "Again?"

"And just exactly what's wrong with hamburgers?" she demanded. The ice came back to her voice.

"Nothing." He sat down across the table from her. "I was just trying to make a little joke. I thought maybe you'd be tired of fixing hamburgers. We've already had them four times this week."

There was laughter in his voice, but Robin ignored it.

"We're having hamburgers, Alex, because that's all we can afford right now." Her entire being trembled. "After all, you want to remember that you don't even have a job."

His face whitened as though she had slapped him.

"For your information," he said hotly, "I've about worn out a pair of shoes walking from one end of this stupid town to the other, trying to find some kind of a job so I could be earning a little money." He straightened. "I don't know why you've decided to be so touchy and hard to get along with all of a sudden. I was just trying to kid with you. I didn't expect you to take what I said seriously."

Her gaze met his.

"Well, please don't try to kid," she said. "I'm not in the mood for it tonight."

"I guess you aren't," he retorted. "It seems to me that you're more in the mood for biting my head off!"

With that they lapsed into silence. It was several minutes before either said a word, and when they did begin to talk again the conversation was taut and strained.

They were just finishing their meal when Robin allowed a smile to rest lightly on her lips.

"I talked with Linda Penner a little while this afternoon," she said.

"So?"

Robin ignored the barb in his voice.

"She asked if we were going to come to Bible club tonight." She hopefully left the question dangling.

Alex shrugged his shoulders.

"Go ahead and go if you want to," he said. "I've got something else to do."

The muscles in her throat tightened even as the lights died in her eyes.

"Please, Alex. Won't you go just this once?"

He shook his head.

"But you promised me."

"I promised that I might go to Bible club with you someday," he said. "I didn't say when."

He got to his feet, stormed into the other room, and dropped heavily into a big chair.

"Hurry and get the dishes done, Robin. I want to go over to my parents' house. This is a good TV night."

Tears came to her eyes, but she quickly wiped them away.

* * *

Several evenings later it was shortly after 6:15 when Alex Smith came home. Robin had been there for almost two hours. She had finished her homework and was in the kitchen fixing supper when he came in.

"Hi, sweetheart." He came over and kissed her on the cheek. "Say, what are you so sad about? Did you burn the hamburgers?"

"It's nothing like that."

"I hope you aren't mad at me."

"It's nothing like that either."

"Then what is it?"

"I've just been a little lonesome. That's all."

"Well, you don't have to be lonesome anymore. I'm here."

She smiled at him. "Now get out of here and let me finish supper, will you?"

Soon she had it ready and on the table. A bit breathlessly she sat down across from her young husband. For the first time he saw that the meal was different. He looked at it appraisingly.

"Say, you sort of outdid yourself tonight, didn't you, Robin?"

A smile played on her lips. "Do you like it?"

"Like it?" he echoed. "I don't know how anyone could help liking a meal like this. It's great!"

Happiness gleamed in her eyes. "I thought you'd enjoy something different than hamburgers for a change."

"You know, I always thought Mom was the best cook in the world, but she couldn't have done a better job than you did on this." He tasted the meat dish once more approvingly. "I tell you, Robin, this is really something."

She was so happy she could cry.

"Thank you, kind sir."

"I've just got one question to ask you. How does it come that you've been holding out on me for so long? Just answer that!"

"I haven't been holding out on you. I just remembered that Kay Orlis fixed this dish once when I was there for a meal. So I called her and got the recipe."

Alex took another helping.

"You'd better call her again and see if she's got another recipe."

"I'm so glad you like it."

Robin went ahead with her plans to have a group of girls over for an evening. Alex hadn't been too excited about it and had talked her into postponing it a time or two, but finally she could be dissuaded no longer. She picked a night and invited a group of the girls she used to run around with.

Just finding a night when there wasn't anything going on at school was difficult enough. Finding a time when all the girls could come was something else again. Robin hadn't realized before she and Alex were married just how many activities there were for the kids who were going to school. At last she settled on a time when most of them could come and called them personally.

For two or three nights before the party Robin worked harder than she had ever worked before. She borrowed her mother's vacuum cleaner and went over the rugs with care. She scrubbed the kitchen floor and washed the windows on the inside. Alex saw the activity and chided her about it.

"Who are you going to entertain?" he asked, chiding her. "The president?"

She paused and wiped the perspiration from her forehead. "I just want our place to look its best when the girls come up. I–I want them to be sure and see how happy we are."

"All I can say," he continued, "is that we ought to have company around here more often."

Robin's eyes grew icy. "Now, what do you mean by that?"

He grinned at her. "Nothing. Nothing at all."

Alex was just teasing her, she knew that. But, in spite of herself, her lower lip trembled. She turned her back on him and set to work furiously.

CHAPTER 11

ALEX HUNTS FOR A JOB

At last the night of the big party arrived. Robin had supper early and as soon as it was over, she shooed Alex out the door.

"You don't mind going over to your parents' this evening, do you?" she asked.

"Of course not. I like to have my wife throw me out of the house."

She made a face at him.

"If you talk like that, I'll take a broom to you."

When he was gone, she stood for a moment in the middle of the kitchen and looked around. She had to frost the cake and do the dishes. Then she could get dressed and wait for her guests.

Everything did look nice if she did say so herself.

Robin had invited the girls for 7:30, but when that time came only Linda Penner was there. Robin glanced uneasily out the living room window.

"I–I thought I made it clear that they were to come tonight."

"Oh, they understood, all right," Linda told her. "I talked with Florence and Sally after school tonight, and they both said they would be coming. But they did think it would be a little late."

"Oh."

"They were planning something for the senior class play."

Robin tried to act as though it didn't really matter what time her guests arrived, but it did. It mattered a great deal.

"I can tell you one thing, Linda," she said in a lame attempt to joke. "After this, I'm never going to be late for anything again."

"I wouldn't worry about them," Linda said. "I'm sure they'll be along in a little while."

It was almost 8:30 when the last of the girls arrived. They came in hesitantly and looked around.

"You have a nice place here, Robin," Florence said. "It's real nice."

"Thank you." She was beginning to feel better, already.

"But, frankly, I didn't think it would be so small." She paused briefly. "I was over at the Park Lane Apartments a couple of weeks ago babysitting. You should have gotten a place there, Robin. Those apartments are absolutely darling. And I think you could have gotten on the ground floor too. You wouldn't have these awful stairs to climb."

One of the other girls broke in. "You really ought to go over and take a look at them. I know that if you just stepped inside one of them and looked around, you'd move over there the first of the month."

"I really want a place like that when I get married," Florence said. "Either an apartment in a building like that or a new home of my own. I think owning a place of your own is far better than even a Park Lane Apartment. That's what you and Alex ought to do, Robin. You should build a house just the way you want it."

Robin's face and neck colored daintily. How could she tell them about the cost of rent and groceries and clothes and–

She felt the muscles in her throat tighten. They could talk. All they knew about money was that when they needed any they went to their parents. With determination she changed the subject.

The girls seemed to have a nice time, but shortly before 10:00 one of the girls looked at her watch. "Oh, I've got to run! Charlie said he was going to call."

Robin eyed her helplessly.

"But we haven't had snacks yet."

"I'm sorry, Robin. Honestly, I am. I couldn't tell you because I knew you don't have a phone."

The color deepened in Robin's cheeks. "I'll fix them right away."

Linda got up and went into the kitchen. "I'll help you."

For a brief instant their eyes met. The corners of Robin's mouth were twitching convulsively.

"They only came because they felt they had to!" Her lips scarcely formed the words.

"I don't think that's it at all, Robin. It's just that the girls are all so busy with things at school and their boyfriends that they don't realize how much work you've gone to. They don't have the slightest idea what it is to fix something like this alone."

When they had finished eating, the other girls by ones and twos got up and excused themselves. In a few minutes Robin and Linda were alone once more. Robin dropped wearily into a big chair. "And I thought they were all my friends," she said miserably.

"They are your friends, Robin."

Her lips quavered.

"They certainly didn't act like it."

"Well–" Linda Penner stopped.

"Well, what?"

There was a short hesitation.

"I–I don't know if I can say exactly what I want to say, Robin," she began, "but when a girl gets married things are different. She's interested in different things than she used to be."

Robin shook her head.

"I don't believe that's true."

Linda's forehead crinkled thoughtfully. "Robin, you were an avid basketball fan a year ago. How many games have you gone to this year?"

She thought about that. "Two, I think. Yes, that's right. We went to two games."

"Did you take part in the cheering? The organized cheering, I mean."

Robin's eyes widened.

"And have everybody laugh at me? I guess not."

"That's just one of the things I'm talking about. It's just like my stepmother told me the other night. When a person is married, whether they like it or not, they move into an entirely different world."

Robin shook her head miserably.

Linda Penner was still at the apartment helping Robin with the dishes when Alex came home shortly after 10:00. He spoke to her and then went into the living room where he sat down and looked at a magazine until Linda left. Then he came to the doorway and stood watching Robin finish cleaning the kitchen.

"How did the party go?" he asked. "I thought the house would still be full of girls when I got here, but I see that it's all over."

"It's all over," she echoed, swallowing at the lump in her throat. "And I'm glad it is."

A strange light gleamed in his eyes. "What happened about the party?"

She was struggling to keep back the tears.

"I think the girls only came because they had to. Everyone, except Linda Penner, came late and left just as early as they possibly could."

"That's too bad. I don't suppose you feel like inviting them back."

She shook her head. "I'm *never* going to ask them to come here again," she said. "It was so–so humiliating."

For a moment or two he looked at her, a grin lighting his young face.

"I don't know what you're finding so funny," she told him.

"I was thinking about something else. You'll never guess what happened tonight."

She hung the dish towel on the rack, walked into the living room, and sat down. "I'm too tired even to try."

"You won't be when I tell you the news." He crossed to the couch and, sitting down, put an arm around her small shoulder.

"Well?" Impatience tinged her voice.

"Dad stopped in at the Highway Service Station this afternoon," Alex said. "He decided to have his oil changed there this time. While he was waiting for the work to be done, the station owner told him that one of his men quit unexpectedly today."

She stared at him.

"You mean–" Words failed her.

"That's right," Alex said. "I called the owner right away and he sounded as though he's really interested in having me come to work for him. I've got an appointment to see him at the station tomorrow at noon.

Robin gasped.

"Alex, it–it hardly seems possible! And after you've looked and looked and looked for work!" Her smile widened. "It's wonderful!"

"You can say that again. Of course I haven't got the job for sure yet, but he sure talked favorably. You know, if I get that job, it won't be long until we'll be able to move out of this dump!"

"Oh, Alex!" Tears came to her eyes. "That's an answer to prayer."

He got to his feet and crossed the room slowly.

"I've never done too much praying, I guess. But if it works at all, you'd better pray now, Robin." His handsome young face grew serious. "I've just got to have this job!"

Robin put the cloth back on the table and put the centerpiece in place. Her heart was singing. Alex was going to get that job! Then they would be able to move to a nicer apartment. She'd show those girls at school. She'd show them!

Alex dressed a little better than usual that morning and, as soon as classes were out at noon, he drove out to the Highway Service Station to talk with the owner. Mr. Pearson visited with him for a few minutes and asked him about his grades in school and for two or three references.

"I'll give you a call tonight and tell you whether I'll be able to use you or not."

"We don't have a phone, Mr. Pearson. W-would it be all right if I call you about 7:30?"

The older man pursed his lips.

"Better make it about 8:00, Alex. I'll know for sure then."

"Thanks!" Alex' eyes brightened. "Thanks a lot." He started for the door but turned back.

"I'm sorry. I almost forgot to ask you. What are the hours that I would be working?"

"The same as the others. You'll be working from 7:00 a.m. until 6:00 p.m. Monday through Saturday. Then you'll have to take your turn working every other Sunday."

Alex's smile faded.

"B-b-but–"

"What's the matter? Don't you want the job?"

"You bet I want the job. I want it more than I ever wanted anything in my whole life. But I–I've got to go to school."

The service station owner shrugged his shoulders.

"Take your pick. Either work for me or go to school. You can't do both."

Robin knew there was something wrong the minute she saw Alex that night after school.

"Did you get the job?" she asked him.

"I don't know yet. To tell you the truth, I don't even know if I'll be able to take it."

"Why not?" Her voice raised.

"Mr. Pearson wants me to work full time. I'd have to quit school."

"Oh–" Her cheeks paled. "That's different."

"I *know* I should be working to support you, but–"

"That's enough of that kind of talk," she told him firmly. "You're going to graduate from high school. That's all there is to it."

"You've had it so hard."

"We aren't going to worry about that," she continued. "When you get out of school, you can look for a full-time job but not until you get your diploma."

He eyed her incredulously. "Do you really mean that, Robin?"

"I certainly do."

He squeezed her arm tenderly. "You're the finest, most wonderful wife a guy could ever have."

At that moment Robin felt as though she could undergo any hardship she was called on to face if it meant that it would please Alex. It was going to be hard for them to get along for a while – until he got out of school, that was. But everything was going to work out for them. She just knew that it was. The sun seemed to be shining a bit warmer as they walked across the parking lot to her car.

THE DANNY ORLIS SERIES

The Danny Orlis series, by Bernard Palmer, delivers a blend of adventure, mystery, and suspense through various settings—from the Canadian wilderness to Guatemalan jungles. Danny Orlis, an adept outdoorsman, skilled athlete, and committed Christian, employs his quick thinking, calm bravery, and biblical solutions to confront everyday problems and hair-raising dangers. Early stories focus on Danny navigating school life, sports, and outdoor challenges, while in later books, Danny and his wife Kay provide wisdom and guidance to youngsters facing lifelike situations and challenges. Having sold over two million copies, this series has made Palmer a renowned author in Christian youth literature. Palmer is also the author of the Felicia Cartright series and various other series for Christian youth.

AVAILABLE FROM WWW.ANEKOPRESS.COM